TOO GOOD TO BE TRUE

A Short Novel

Nikita Zabzine

ISBN: 978-91-531-8565-9

Cover design by: Nikita Zabzine
Published by: Nikita Zabzine, Stockholm, Sweden

Printed in the United States of America

"Man is condemned to be free; because once thrown into the world, he is responsible for everything he does."

JEAN-PAUL SARTRE

Chapter 1

THE PHASE

The room had not changed much since he was seventeen. The same narrow bed. The same desk pressed against the wall. The same Barack Obama poster above it, the words "*Yes We Can*" faded now, the corners curling as if optimism itself had grown tired of staying.

The only difference was Andy himself, who had grown into the space badly, like a plant kept too long in the wrong pot.

There was a time when Andy had said farewell to his teenage room with a glint in his eye and hopes for a wonderful future. A future filled with a successful career and exciting experiences. He had left to study at business school, convinced that this was the beginning of something permanent.

Now he was back, occupying the room he had once said goodbye to. He was rich in knowledge, but poor in every way that mattered. The Master of Business Administration or MBA he had worked so hard to obtain hung on the wall beside the curled-up poster. Framed. Official. A quiet reminder of how society had sold him a lie.

He laid on his bed with his phone resting against his chest, scrolling through Instagram reels of flashy lifestyles in Dubai. Then LinkedIn, where people posted about career successes and how simple moments in life had taught them everything they knew about business-to-business sales, often followed by long explanations from boomers about why Gen Z was lazy.

Meanwhile, Andy searched frantically for jobs.

Jobs that were fake.

Jobs that ghosted.

It had been two years since Andy received his degree. Two years of scrolling through LinkedIn and job boards. Over five hundred applications, and only five interviews, each ending with the same cold sentence:

We've decided to move forward with another candidate.

After his MBA, Andy had been unemployed, aside from a six-month internship at a large firm. The internship took more than it gave. More time. More energy. More money. Without leading to a permanent position or even useful experience.

Most mornings, Andy woke up already tired. Not physically, but in the way that came from anticipating explanations. Explanations to his mother. To old friends. To former classmates. To Tinder dates, potential partners who had learned to ask the question "So, what are you doing in life?" with careful politeness, as if it were a medical condition.

His phone was rarely silent. It vibrated with bank notifications, promotional emails, reminders from apps he no longer remembered downloading. What it did not do was ring with opportunity. Andy refreshed his inbox often enough that it felt like a tic. Like a smoker stepping outside for another cigarette. Each refresh was a small negotiation with hope.

Downstairs, his mother moved through the kitchen with the quiet efficiency of someone who had learned not to make noise where noise might invite explanation. She did not ask about his job search; she already knew the answer. Instead, she asked if he wanted eggs for breakfast.

Andy always said yes.

Eggs were uncomplicated.

He put on his bathrobe and shuffled down the stairs. He sat at the kitchen table while his mother placed a plate of fried eggs beside him, kissed his forehead, and rushed off to work.

She wore a dark grey suit with a white blouse, pressed and practical, the kind of outfit chosen once and then replicated without variation. Since divorcing Andy's father, she had held two jobs: one was taking care of Andy, the other was being head of accounting at a law firm.

She had worked her way up through experience and trust, learning systems by repetition rather than theory, numbers by use rather than abstraction.

She had never opened a university textbook. Never studied business, leadership models, or motivational frameworks. She had not needed to. Her authority came from competence, not credentials. From showing up every day and not failing publicly.

Higher education had become an obligatory step for younger generations, a toll paid in advance for the possibility of stability. A prerequisite that promised access but delivered uncertainty.

But it had never applied to her.

Not to her generation. She had arrived before the gate was built.

Andy watched her through the window as she got into her car, parked in the driveway with efficient familiarity, already dressed for a world that still made sense to her.

He had done everything right.

And still, he was here.

Andy thought life was unfair.

He ate his breakfast at the kitchen table, scrolling through social media with one hand and holding his fork in the other. His feed was full of people his age announcing engagements, promotions, apartments with suspiciously large windows. He liked the photos automatically, his thumb trained to perform encouragement even when his face did not.

Every post promised *la dolce vita*.

Perfect versions of themselves.

Sometimes he imagined his own post: a desk, a laptop, a caption that implied purpose. He did not imagine the work itself, only the proof of it. Evidence that he was somewhere in his little life.

Andy was not unhappy. He was not depressed. What he felt instead was a low, constant pressure, like being underwater without knowing how deep you were. Time behaved differently there. Days blurred. Weeks became administrative units rather than experiences.

The Barack Obama poster still hung above his desk.

Yes we can.

Once, it had felt inspiring. A promise of momentum. Of progress. Now it read more like an artefact from another era: a future that had been imagined and quietly replaced by the need to make something great again, whatever that was supposed to mean.

He told himself this feeling was normal. Everyone he knew seemed to live inside the same quiet tension, or at least the internet suggested they did. Entire articles and TikToks existed to reassure him that his life was not a failure, merely a *phase*.

Andy liked the word *phase*.

It implied an end.

Still.

He felt he could do better. On social media, others appeared to be living proof that improvement was not only possible, but expected.

In the evenings, he lay on his bed with his phone resting on his chest, watching other people live convincingly edited lives. He was good at noticing details: the lighting, the angles, the way success was framed as effortless. He filed these observations away without knowing why.

Andy was single. He had never had many girlfriends, just a few. His most recent relationship, from university, had ended a year earlier.

They had been together for barely three years. At his age, it had felt like a lifetime. When the relationship finally began to run on fumes, it was his ex-girlfriend who initiated the breakup. She explained it to herself by deciding that Andy was a loser without a future.

To reassure herself, she convinced herself that she could not be with someone who was unemployed and living at his mother's house, even though she, too, was unemployed and living at home. She also told herself she was too young to settle down, that she needed to find her path.

Andy recognised the explanation for what it was: reassurance disguised as resolve.

She left him soon after, travelling to Bali to find herself.

Andy, meanwhile, was keen on being in a relationship with someone.

He spent time on dating apps like Hinge and Tinder. He went on a few dates, many of which ended either after he had paid for dinner or with a one-night stand followed by silence.

He felt that dating was brutal. People showed up carrying unrealistic expectations of one another. The girl was supposed to be effortlessly attractive.

The guy had to be physically fit, witty in his messages, and already well settled mentally and financially.

Online dating felt as depressing as looking for a job in the modern, no, postmodern era. An era where people no longer believed in facts but instead produced their own truths, confidently and without consequence. Everyone clung to their personal version of reality, insisting it was universal.

His phone chimed.

A notification.

It was a match.

Her name was Charlotte.

She was twenty-four.

She was beautiful: lustrous chestnut hair, blue eyes that carried a feeling of warmth and comfort. In every photo Andy swiped past, she smiled. The smile felt new, and yet strangely familiar.

Andy fell in love with the photos.

Her caption read:

Good coffee, long walks, bad jokes.

It made Andy chuckle.

Knowing she was out of his league, he kept it simple. He typed a sparse message:

Hello, Charlotte.

What did he have to lose?

Chapter 2

THE FIRST DATE

Andy did not expect a reply from Charlotte. He sent the message and placed his phone face down on the bed, as if avoiding eye contact might make rejection less personal. He had learned, over time, that some things felt safer when left unseen.

He lay staring at the ceiling, telling himself that this was nothing, that he had sent worse messages and survived.

The phone buzzed.

Andy picked it up, already assuming it wasn't her. The odds were low. He immediately regretted not putting more effort into his first message, maybe a joke, maybe something clever about her caption. There was a familiar, dull regret.

The Uber app was offering thirty percent off his next trip.

Andy sighed and tossed the phone lightly to the other side of the bed.

The phone buzzed again.

Hi Andy :)

No way.

That was it. No punctuation beyond the emoji. No questions. No measurable effort. Andy read it three times, each reading slightly different from the last. Still, his expectations remained low. Plenty of people had answered hello with hello before, only to disappear later.

He replied too quickly.

How are you today, Charlotte?

Immediately, he realised it wasn't enough. There might be a chance here. Panicking slightly, he followed up.

Do you like kangaroos? :)

The moment he pressed send, regret set in.

Kangaroos?

Who writes that?

Charlotte replied almost immediately.

I'm fine :) How are you?

Hmm... kangaroos? That's not an animal that usually comes to mind. I think I like them.

Andy smirked.

They exchanged messages the way people do when both are trying not to seem too invested. Short sentences. Carefully placed pauses. Light jokes that could be withdrawn without embarrassment if they failed to land.

Charlotte wrote with an economy Andy found calming. No long explanations. No over-sharing. She used emojis sparingly, just enough to soften a sentence without turning it into performance. Andy read this as maturity. As emotional control. As someone who had learned, perhaps the hard way, not to offer too much too soon.

She laughed at his jokes, not every one, but the right ones. Andy read that as chemistry. As timing. As proof that he was saying the right things. Each small affirmation landed heavily, filling the spaces where doubt usually lived.

She asked what he did.

Andy paused.

He lay back on the bed, phone balanced on his chest, feeling the familiar tightening in his stomach. The question was harmless. It always was. And yet it felt like a test he had already failed too many times.

I work in finance, he typed.

It wasn't entirely untrue. He had studied finance. He understood the language. He knew what the words meant.

After a moment, he deleted finance and replaced it with consulting. It sounded better. Broader. Like a word that could stretch without breaking.

Consulting, he sent.

Charlotte replied almost immediately.

Oh, nice! That sounds interesting.

Andy exhaled. Interesting was good. Interesting meant he could stay where he was without being examined too closely.

What do you do? Andy wrote.

I work at a preschool with children.

Wow, that's even more interesting than my job, Andy replied, genuinely impressed.

What does a consultant do? Charlotte asked.

Without hesitation, Andy answered.

A consultant consults.

Charlotte replied instantly.

Hahaha, no, silly. I know that. What do you actually do?

Andy's stomach dropped. He fully understood now that he had lied. And now that the conversation was going so well, he couldn't tell the truth without collapsing everything they had built in the last hour.

So, he lied again.

I'm a financial consultant.

Wow, that's cool, Charlotte replied.

You must make a lot of money.

She simply assumed that financial consultants made good money.

So, what does a financial consultant do? she asked.

I consult companies on their financial portfolios, Andy replied. *And I get a cut of the profits if the portfolios perform well.*

Andy knew he was lying. But this. This connection felt rare. And rare things, he told himself, deserved protection. Even if that protection came at a cost he refused to calculate yet.

Right then, without fully acknowledging it, he decided to continue being this version of himself. He told himself it was temporary. He did not ask what temporary usually turned into. What he did not know then was that he had dug himself into a rabbit hole.

They moved off the app that same evening. Instagram first, then WhatsApp. Andy watched as Charlotte followed him, then quickly scrolled through his own profile, seeing it through her eyes. The photos were carefully chosen: nothing flashy, nothing poor. A coffee on a wooden table. A city skyline from a trip years ago. A photo with him in a suit from a wedding that could easily pass for a business event.

Charlotte's Instagram felt warmer. Friends. Sunlight. Dinners that looked casual rather than staged. She seemed real in a way that made Andy nervous.

They agreed to meet for drinks later that week.

Andy spent the next three days preparing.

Not for conversation, he was good at that, but for context. He researched the bar she suggested, Janus and the Glass, checking the price range and the interior. Dim lighting. Youthful crowd. Acceptable.

He checked his bank account. It was running on fumes. He transferred what little savings he had left and imagined his card beeping insufficient funds in front of her.

As insurance, he applied for a credit card.

The people at the firm he once was an intern at, all had American Express cards.

He applied.

It would take a week to arrive, but his application was approved immediately. A welcoming email congratulated him on becoming a Premium cardholder.

He hadn't felt this excited about anything in a long time. The feeling was sharp and clean, like relief, but it didn't last long enough to feel safe.

Still, he needed something faster. He applied for a basic MasterCard with airline miles and received it the next day.

On the evening of the date, he stood in front of the mirror longer than usual, adjusting his shirt, rolling his sleeves up and down, trying to find the version of himself that looked like it belonged somewhere else.

He considered wearing the suit from his internship but decided the bar was too casual. Business casual would do.

His mother called from downstairs, asking where he was going.

"Out with friends," Andy said.

She didn't question it. She was simply glad he was going out.

Andy arrived ten minutes early and ordered an expensive draft beer he didn't particularly like because it felt appropriate. He paid with his new MasterCard, its airline logo catching the light.

Charlotte arrived right on time.

She scanned the room, squinting slightly at each man she passed.

Andy smiled at her. She smiled back and walked towards him.

She was even more beautiful in person. The smile from her photos was real. It landed easily, as if it had practiced landing on people.

"Andy?" she asked.

Nervous, he stood too quickly, nearly knocking over his chair.

"That's me," he said, smiling wider than necessary.

They hugged sparsely and sat at the bar.

"So," Charlotte exclaimed nervously, spreading her arms, "here we are."

"Yeah," Andy replied. "I'm sorry, you probably get this a lot..."

"Get what?" she interrupted.

Andy chuckled. "But you're very beautiful tonight."

Charlotte blushed. "Oh, what a flirt."

"No one's ever said that to me on a first date," she added.

"Do you really think I'm beautiful?" she asked.

"Yes," Andy said.

"Beautiful is such a strong word," Charlotte said. "It's like saying I love you..."

An awkward silence followed.

"I don't mean it like that," she said quickly. "Well.... no"

"Let's just skip that part," Andy said.

"Which part?" she asked. "That I'm beautiful?"

"Oh god, no," Andy said. "That part stays. I'm just flabbergasted by your beauty."

They laughed.

Conversation came easily after that. Charlotte made Andy feel clever and funny. She leaned forward when he spoke. She laughed with her whole face.

"Did you come here from work?" she asked.

"No, from home," Andy replied instinctively, then corrected himself. "I worked from home today."

"Lucky you," Charlotte said. "I have to be at the preschool every day, seven to four."

"Yeah," Andy said, with a pause. "How was your day?"

"Fine. Well-behaved kids."

"Cool."

"I think you have the most interesting job at this table," Charlotte said. "Can you tell me more about it?"

Andy laughed softly, feeling the weight of how far the lie had gone. For a moment, he considered telling the truth.

"Well... here's the thing," he started.

Charlotte leaned closer, her blue eyes warm and attentive. She wore a dark dress, black, maybe navy, hard to tell in the dim light. The neckline dipped slightly, and as she leaned in, Andy's focus faltered.

Her two breasts squeezed tightly inside the push-up bra she was wearing underneath her dress. Fresh. With a small birthmark on the left breast.

Blood left his head.

He thought naughty thoughts of what he could do with them.

He changed his mind.

"Well," he continued with some pause, "I help

clients with their investment portfolios."

"So you're like an investment banker?" she asked.

"Not really," Andy said. "I help companies optimise their portfolios and maximise profits."

"Oh, cool," Charlotte said, not fully understanding.

Andy sensed her uncertainty and filled the space with confident nonsense.

"It's mostly project-based," he said. "Different clients. Keeps things interesting."

"That sounds fun," Charlotte said. "I like people who don't do the same thing every day."

Andy nodded, storing that sentence carefully.

They ordered another round and some food. Charlotte accepted that she wouldn't fully understand his job and maybe that was fine. She wanted to know him, not his CV.

Andy watched the total climb and refused to look directly at the bill. He told himself this was an investment.

When the check arrived, he grabbed it before Charlotte could.

"You sure?" she asked.

"Of course," Andy said. "I've got it."

In that small, unremarkable moment, something shifted. The lie no longer felt like a lie. It felt like movement. And movement, once started, was difficult to stop without falling.

Outside, Charlotte hugged him goodbye.

Andy didn't want it to end there. He pulled her

closer and kissed her.

She froze for a second, then melted into it.

“I’d like to see you again,” she said.

“So would I,” Andy replied, without hesitation.

On the walk home, he felt lighter than he had in months. His phone buzzed before he reached the corner.

I had a really nice time.

Andy stopped on the sidewalk, smiling at the screen while people passed around him.

For the first time in a long while, his life felt like it was starting.

He did not think about the bill.

He did not think about his bank account.

He did not think about how many times he would have to repeat the story he had just begun telling.

That could wait.

Andy had always been good at postponing things that frightened him. He told himself there would be time later, when everything made more sense. When the story matched the facts.

INTERLUDE 1

Charlotte

Charlotte walked home slowly, even though the cold had started to bite.

She wanted the fresh air, the movement, the uninterrupted space to replay the evening without distraction. Walking helped her organise feelings before they became expectations.

Andy had been kind. That was the word that stayed with her. Not charming. Not impressive. Kind. He listened when she spoke, laughed without checking whether anyone else was watching. He paid attention in a way that felt intentional, as if she mattered specifically, not just in theory.

That counted for more than most things.

She passed shop windows along the street, each one reflecting a softened version of her, blurred by glass, fractured by light. She caught her own reflection once, then lost it again as the angle shifted.

The kiss lingered in her thoughts. It hadn't been perfect, not technically, but it had been right. Contextually right. Perfect in retrospect, even if it had been slightly awkward while it happened.

She could still feel his hand in hers, a little damp shaking with nerves, the odd angle of her arm as he leaned in, the brief discomfort of bodies adjusting too late. It hadn't flowed. It had happened.

And yet.

It had been decisive. Confident. As if he had known exactly when to do it. That was what made it attractive. Charlotte liked that. She was tired of being the one who nudged things forward, who waited patiently for men to realise they were allowed to want her.

Still, something about him felt… arranged.

Not false. Just curated.

She thought about the way he spoke about his job. Like it was the only thing he did, work. The confidence. The smooth transitions. The lack of specifics. It registered, but it didn't alarm her. People with white-collar jobs often spoke like that. She had dated enough men with impressive-sounding titles and vague realities to know that clarity was rarely part of the package.

Andy felt safe. Like someone who wouldn't disappear suddenly. He filled silences without rushing them, without turning every pause into a performance.

And still, there had been moments. Small ones. Flickers. When she felt as though she was interacting with a surface rather than a depth. Like seeing a reflection instead of the object itself.

She noticed it. Filed it away. First dates were

not meant for conclusions.

She lived close to Janus & the Glass, and soon she found herself standing outside her apartment building. Her hand drifted instinctively toward her phone.

What if he had already written?

He hadn't.

Messages from friends stacked her notifications instead, variations of: *How was it? Tell us everything.*

She smiled, embarrassed by how much she wanted to answer them honestly.

Inside her apartment, she kicked off her shoes and hung her coat carefully, the way she always did. She poured herself a glass of water and leaned against the kitchen counter, letting the room settle around her.

She typed: *I had a really nice time.*

She didn't add an emoji. She wanted it to stand on its own.

Almost immediately, three dots appeared.

A quiet excitement bloomed in her chest: small, controlled, familiar.

She told herself not to read into it. Everyone was attentive at the beginning. Everyone was thoughtful while they were still choosing.

She got ready for bed, brushing her teeth, tying her hair back. And without intending to, she wondered what Andy's apartment looked like. Whether it was tidy or cluttered. Whether he lived alone.

Her thoughts drifted forward, too far forward. A future version of herself. A vague ceremony. A dress she hadn't chosen.

She stopped, pressed her palm briefly to her forehead, and let out a breath.

She knew this pattern.

Still, one thing felt true.

She liked him.

And from experience, she knew that liking someone was never the uncomplicated part; it was the beginning of the work.

Chapter 3

THE UPGRADE

Andy woke up before his alarm. That alone felt like progress.

For once, the first thing he thought about was not his inbox, or the quiet weight of another unstructured day. It was Charlotte. Her smile. The calm brightness of her blue eyes. The way her attention had settled on him, unhurried, as if she had nowhere else to be. The message she had sent him after the date.

I had a really nice time.

He reread it while lying on his back, phone held above his face, the green glow soft against the half-light of his room. The ceiling above him was the same one he had stared at for years, but the thought beneath it felt new.

He waited before replying. Not because he didn't want to answer, he did, but because wanting too much felt dangerous. Desperation had a smell. He had learned that.

Eventually, he typed:

Me too.

Did you sleep well?

Downstairs, his mother was already awake. The smell of coffee and fried eggs drifted up the stairs, briefly grounding him in a reality he didn't want to enter yet. He pulled on a clean shirt, not special, just intentional, and went down to the kitchen.

"You're in a good mood," his mother said, not looking up from the counter.

"Yeah," Andy replied. "Went out yesterday."

"That's nice," she said, and meant it. It was nice to see him animated again, even if she didn't ask for details.

He ate the breakfast she had prepared, one hand on his fork, the other on his phone. Quietly. His mother moved around the kitchen with practised efficiency, tidying, getting ready for work. They had learned how to coexist without pressing too much against each other.

He finished quickly and went back to his room.

He told himself he would apply for jobs today.

By noon, Charlotte had replied.

Their conversation resumed easily, lightly, as if nothing fragile were being built beneath it.

How is your day? Charlotte wrote.

Andy waited a few minutes before answering. Timing mattered.

Good. Busy. He replied.

Oh, you must have a lot on your plate.

Yeah. Project deadline today. Clients calling to

check in.

Sounds stressful.

It is. But it's the usual grind.

As he typed, the words came more easily than they should have. He wasn't inventing so much as borrowing phrases overheard at his previous internship, half-remembered complaints from people who had places to be. The language of work had always been available to him, even if the work itself had not.

That afternoon, Andy went shopping. With his new credit card.

He told himself it was overdue. That clothes mattered. That presentation mattered. People saw you before they knew you. Employers. Women. Everyone.

The store was quiet, softly lit. The kind of place where nothing had visible logos, where the sales assistants spoke calmly, as if rushing would be vulgar. Andy moved through the racks slowly, touching fabrics, checking seams, learning how quality announced itself quietly.

He chose a shirt first. Crisp, well-fitted. The kind of white that wasn't very white, softened just enough to suggest expense. Then trousers that sat properly at the waist, jackets that structured his shoulders without exaggerating them. Shoes with weight to them. Presence.

Nothing flashy. Flashy was suspicious.

He stood in front of the mirror in the fitting room, adjusting the collar, turning slightly to see himself from different angles. He recognised the man looking back at him, but only partially. This version stood straighter. Looked like someone who arrived somewhere in the morning and left somewhere in the evening.

He imagined Charlotte noticing the details. Not consciously. Just feeling it. The ease of being with someone who seemed established. Secure.

He paid with his new credit card, barely registering the total. The number didn't feel real yet. It lived somewhere abstract, future bound.

He told himself it was practical.

An investment.

Clothes, after all, were visible proof. You could wear success before you earned it. You could borrow credibility, just long enough for reality to catch up.

One day, he would pay it all back.

One day, the clothes would match the life.

For now, he folded the receipts into his pocket, already thinking about what he would wear when he saw Charlotte again.

Andy hung the new clothes carefully in his wardrobe, spacing them out as if they needed room to breathe. They looked almost out of place among the older shirts, like guests who had arrived early to a party that hadn't quite begun.

He sat back on his bed and checked his phone.

A message from Charlotte.

What are you up to tonight?

Andy smiled before answering.

Nothing special. Just a quiet evening. You?

The three dots appeared almost immediately.

I was thinking...

He waited; heart ticking faster than it should.

There's this Italian restaurant I went to last week with my friend Sabrina, she wrote.

It was really nice. Cozy. Good pasta.

He could picture it already: candlelight, wine glasses, linen napkins. Her beautiful face lit by the candles on the table.

Would you like to go there with me? Maybe later this week?

Andy stared at the screen for a moment, letting the words settle.

She was asking him.

I'd love to, he replied. *That sounds perfect :)*

A pause.

Then:

Great :) Friday?

Friday works.

He set the phone down and leaned back, exhaling slowly.

Somewhere beneath the excitement, something else stirred, quiet, barely formed. The awareness that this was no longer just chance. That with each step forward, something unseen was also being built.

Outside, the late afternoon light faded gently into evening, and Andy lay there imagining red wine, shared plates, Charlotte's laughter across a small table.

He didn't think about the cost.

He didn't think about what he would wear; he already knew.

And he didn't think about how carefully the story would need to be told next time.

For now, it was enough to be chosen again.

Chapter 4

THE BEDROCK

Their second date came quickly. Dinner this time, Charlotte's suggestion.

They met outside the restaurant just after seven. The windows glowed warmly against the early evening, the inside already busy with soft voices and clinking glasses.

Charlotte arrived first. When Andy spotted her, something in his chest lifted involuntarily.

She wore a simple coat, open at the collar, her chestnut hair loose around her shoulders. Her blue eyes caught the light when she smiled at him, promising comfort rather than excitement, which somehow felt more dangerous.

"Hi," she said.

"Hi," Andy replied, leaning in for a hug that lasted half a second longer than necessary.

"You found it easily?" she asked.

"Yeah," he said. "You have good taste."

She smiled at that, pleased but not surprised.

Inside, they were shown to a small table near the wall. The space felt intimate without trying. Candles flickered. Plates of pasta passed them, steaming, fragrant.

They sat down.

The waiter appeared almost immediately.

"Can I get you started with something to drink?"

Andy didn't hesitate. "We'll share a bottle of the Pinot Grigio, please."

Charlotte raised her eyebrows, amused. "Only if you want to."

"I do," Andy said, smiling at her. And he meant it, not just the wine, but the decision to choose without asking.

"Then yes," she said. "That sounds perfect."

The waiter, awaiting the table's consensus, nodded and disappeared.

"So," Charlotte said, folding her hands together on the table. "How was your day?"

Andy exhaled softly. "Long."

She tilted her head. "Busy-long or boring-long?"

"Busy," he said. "The kind where you don't notice the time passing until it's already evening."

She nodded as if she understood exactly.

"I had one of those too," she said. "Except mine involved a four-year-old crying because someone else got the blue cup."

Andy laughed. "That sounds… intense."

"It was," she said solemnly. "We survived."

As she talked, Andy watched the way her face changed with the story. How her voice softened when she spoke about the children. How invested she was.

"There was this one boy," she said, smiling. "He finally tied his shoes today. He looked at me like he'd just won an Olympic medal."

"That's huge," Andy said. "You should've given him a podium."

"I considered it," she laughed. "But we settled for applause."

The wine arrived, and for a moment their conversation paused as the waiter filled their glasses.

"To second dates," Charlotte said, lifting her glass.

"To good Italian restaurants," Andy replied.

They clinked glasses.

Conversation flowed more easily now. Less careful. Less edited. They spoke over each other sometimes, laughed without checking whether it was appropriate, let silences sit without filling them immediately.

Charlotte asked questions the way people do when they're genuinely curious, not interrogating. Andy found himself answering more freely than he'd planned.

"And you?" she asked eventually. "How's work?"

There it was.

Andy took a sip of wine, buying himself a moment.

"It's... busy," he said again, expanding smoothly. "A lot of overlapping projects right now."

"That sounds stressful," she said.

"It can be," Andy replied. "But I like the pace. It keeps things interesting."

"What kind of projects?" she asked, leaning forward slightly.

Andy smiled, the story already forming.

"Well," he began, and let the lie stretch just a little further than before.

His fictitious job became the center of him. He built the version of Andy he presented around it. His real life felt thin now, and the lie gave him shape. And somehow, inside the false words, something real still lived.

He wasn't cruel. He was adapting. He feared losing her.

He talked about clients, timelines, pressure. About long days and blurred boundaries. He borrowed phrases from podcasts, articles, conversations overheard in cafés.

Charlotte listened, impressed but not intimidated.

"That sounds stressful," she said.

"It can be," Andy replied. "But it's rewarding."

And in that moment, it almost felt true.

"As a consultant," Charlotte asked, "are you self-employed or with a firm?"

Andy felt a flash of panic. The questions were becoming specific. For a brief, uncomfortable second, he thought of the men, alpha-bros, online who claimed women only cared about money.

"You ask a lot about my job," he said.

"Well, it's all you talk about," Charlotte replied gently.

"Do you have any hobbies?" she continued.

Andy didn't. Not really.

"I work at a consulting firm," he said, quickly choosing a name he admired. "Perspective Capital Partners. PCP."

Her eyes widened. "That's impressive. The one with the skyscraper downtown?"

"Yes," Andy said. "Headquartered in Geneva. Global affiliates."

He surprised himself with how smoothly it came out.

"And what do you do when you're not working?" she asked. "Or do you just work all the time?"

"I play golf," Andy said, then immediately regretted it.

He never played golf.

"That's boring," Charlotte said, then winced. "Sorry. I didn't mean..."

"I'm joking," Andy said quickly, feeling the momentum slip.

"No, it's fine," she said. "You don't need a hobby. I'll stop asking."

"I play tennis," Andy said suddenly, remembering the racket still hanging unused in his teenage room.

"That's something I'd like to try," Charlotte said.

Andy felt hope spark. "We could play sometime."

After dinner, they walked through the city. At night, it felt softer, quieter, as if it belonged only to them.

Andy walked her home in a gentlemanly manner, respectful.

As days progressed, they started seeing each other more often. Coffee before her shifts. Casual drinks after.

He posted on social media occasionally. Nothing obvious. Charlotte liked every photo.

That mattered.

At home, the credit card balance crept upward.

Andy noticed, briefly, then closed the app.

He told himself it would even out once he got a job. That this was temporary. That everyone lived like this at first.

Eventually, Charlotte invited him to stay over one night at her place. Her version of approval.

Her apartment was small but careful. One main room that held her bed, sofa, kitchen, and dining table. A bathroom. A tiny separate room squeezed into being a home office.

The furniture was second-hand, mostly from the fifties and sixties. Nothing minimalist. Frames everywhere with photos of friends, family, different ages, different moments stacked, leaning, overlapping.

"Sorry if it's messy," Charlotte said, pushing

her hoodie off the sofa.

They sat down. She asked if he wanted to watch something.

Instead, Andy leaned in and kissed her.

One kiss. Then another. Then one that lasted too long to count.

As they kissed, Charlotte rested her hand against his chest, steady and warm. Andy's fingers found the hem of her black top, and for a moment they hesitated, smiling softly, as if checking that they were moving at the same pace. Then the fabric was gone, discarded without ceremony.

He took a second longer than necessary, to admire her bosom. Breasts ripe and firm. Committing the moment to memory, before drawing her closer again.

The kiss deepened. Whatever remained between them: clothes, distance, caution, fell away as they moved together toward the bed, leaving only a quiet trail of clothes behind them.

As she lay on the bed, her body open and trusting, Andy kissed her slowly, deliberately, as if learning her rather than claiming her. From her neck downward, his attention unhurried, attentive, each touch an affirmation rather than a demand.

When they bonded together, it felt less like urgency and more like recognition. Andy above her, their bodies moving in a quiet conversation, careful and present. It was tender, charged not by haste but by intention.

Charlotte shifted, finding her own rhythm,

her hands resting against his chest as if grounding herself there. He followed her pace, attentive to every change in breath, every subtle response. Feeling the hidden pearl with his thumb, gently. There was a moment where control dissolved entirely, where sensation overtook thought, and she let go without warning. Shaking.

They lay still, the intensity giving way to something softer, almost reverent. It felt less like an ending than a release, like something carried on the air and scattered gently, leaving only calm behind.

Later, lying beside her in the softly lit room, Andy felt overwhelmed, not by doubt, but by disbelief. It had been good. More than good. A warmth that stayed with him, humming through his body.

Her blue eyes looked even more striking in the low light.

"Should we sleep?" she asked.

He agreed.

She turned off the lights. They couldn't see each other, but they could feel each other. It was comforting. Anchoring.

As Andy held her, the low hum of anxiety returned, quieter than before, but heavier. No longer sharp enough to interrupt him. Now it simply existed.

When Charlotte fell asleep, her breathing slow and even, Andy checked his phone one last time. A bank notification. A reminder. An offer for a higher credit limit.

He put the phone away.

Tomorrow, he told himself, he would apply for jobs properly. Really commit. Fix things.

But tomorrow felt abstract.

Right now, Charlotte was beside him.

Right now, he looked like the man he wanted to be.

And for the first time, Andy wondered... just briefly, whether it mattered which version of him was real.

Somewhere else in the city, his mother wondered where Andy was, and when he would be coming home.

INTERLUDE 2

His Mother

She woke up with the alarm, the way she always did.

The house was quiet. Too quiet for a place meant to hold two adults and a future. She moved through the kitchen carefully.

Andy's door was closed.

She noticed these things. Doors. Shoes. The absence of small noises. She had learned not to ask questions that already had answers.

She placed an espresso capsule into the machine and stood at the counter as she waited for her coffee to brew. Looking out at the street as it began to hum. People walked with purpose. Coats buttoned. Bags slung over shoulders. Mornings that moved forward whether you were ready or not.

Andy hadn't come home.

That was new, at least since he had moved back.

She tried not to dwell on it, but change unsettled her more than she liked to admit. Routine was safety.

To calm herself, she reminded herself that Andy was an adult and not a child anymore. He was allowed a life of his own.

Still.

She thought about Andy as a child. Quiet. Observant. The kind of boy who noticed when voices changed, when moods shifted. He had never been demanding. Never loud. Even then, he seemed careful not to take up space.

His father used to call him "easy."

She had never liked that word.

His father believed in effort. In discipline. In the promise that if you worked hard enough, life would eventually meet you halfway. He had built his career step by step and expected the world to reward the same discipline in others.

When it didn't, he took it personally.

The divorce hadn't been dramatic. No shouting. No slammed doors. Just exhaustion. Two people realising that love, stretched thin for too long, didn't break, it thinned.

She felt that Andy had taken it harder than he ever admitted.

After the divorce, his father moved on quickly. New wife. New house. New car. Forward motion as proof of success. Standing still was failure.

Andy came home after university. In his father's logic, that alone was defeat, ignoring the housing market, the cost-of-living crisis, the world his generation had helped create.

She told herself it was fine. Children always

came back for a while. The job market was difficult. An MBA was a good thing.

And it was. At least according to institutions that still spoke in outdated certainties.

She saw how carefully Andy dressed when he went out. How vaguely he spoke about his job search. How he avoided details. How he smiled just enough. It felt less like struggle and more like surrender.

They didn't talk much because neither of them wanted to ask the wrong question.

She didn't want to hear that he was stuck.

He didn't want to hear that she was worried.

She had done everything she thought she was supposed to do. Encouraged education. Stability. Responsibility. She had believed, honestly, fervently, that if you worked hard, stayed polite, didn't cause trouble, life would eventually meet you halfway.

That was how it had worked for her.

She had grown up being told that effort mattered. That degrees opened doors. That patience and loyalty were rewarded. That adulthood was something you arrived at naturally, like a station you reached on time.

Somewhere along the way, that stopped being true.

She watched Andy do everything right and still end up nowhere. Watched him collect qualifications that never turned into security. Watched him retreat into politeness, into vagueness, into a version of himself that spoke carefully but said very little.

Sometimes she wondered if she had failed him by preparing him for a world that no longer existed.

She didn't understand his generation very well. Their exhaustion confused her. Their anger frightened her. The way everything seemed harder and more fragile at the same time. She read articles about them: about anxiety, burnout, hopelessness and felt a quiet shame recognising her own son between the lines.

She had thought love and encouragement would be enough.

Sometimes she sensed resentment in Andy. That she hadn't done enough. That she should have known better.

She finished her coffee and checked the time. She had to leave.

She picked up her bag, locked the door behind her, and stepped into the morning.

Somewhere in the city, her son was asleep in someone else's bed, trying to become the version of himself he believed the world would accept.

Or he was lying dead in a bush.

For insurance, she took out her phone and typed:

Andy, when are you coming home? xx Mum

Chapter 5

THE GRAND HOTEL

Andy woke up in Charlotte's bed. He could smell her almond shampoo on the pillow and the faint freshness of newly washed sheets.

Charlotte was nowhere to be seen. Somewhere nearby, coffee was brewing.

She emerged from the bathroom wearing Andy's shirt from the night before, unbuttoned, the cotton brushing against her bare legs as she moved through the room. Andy watched her, still half-asleep, and felt a quiet, uncomplicated desire settle in his chest.

"Good morning, sleepyhead," Charlotte said, sitting down beside him on the bed.

"Good morning," Andy replied.

"When do you need to get to work?" she asked.

"Work?" Andy repeated.

She laughed softly. “Not a morning person, I see,” she said, kissing his forehead.

For a brief second, Andy slipped out of character. He realised he needed to invent a schedule.

He reached for his phone on the bedside table. As he checked the time, he noticed a message from his mother. Charlotte caught a glimpse of the message on the screen.

“Are you visiting your mum today?” she asked.

“Uh... yes,” Andy said after a pause.

“That’s sweet,” Charlotte said. “Do you have any siblings?”

“Not really. Just a half-brother on my dad’s side.”

Without warning, Charlotte slipped out of the shirt, exposing herself to the cool morning air. Her pale breast reflecting the morning light. Andy didn’t think; he pulled her gently towards him and kissed her, long and lingering.

“I have to get ready for work,” she said eventually. “And so do you.”

They dressed and ate breakfast mostly in silence. Not an uncomfortable one, just the kind that didn’t need filling.

Outside, they kissed goodbye and headed in opposite directions. Charlotte briefly noticed that Andy walked the other way than she expected, given where his office supposedly was. She dismissed it quickly; perhaps he was picking something up, perhaps seeing a client.

Andy walked toward the bus stop instead, irritated by his mother's message. It made him feel younger than he wanted to be. He replied:

I'm on my way home now. I stayed over at a friend.

On the bus, he replayed the night. It had been good, almost unreal, even if he'd barely slept. His arm had gone numb more than once. He smiled at the memory. First sleepovers were always like that. Awkward. Unnatural. A beginning.

She held him without asking anything of him. Her touch was calm, assured, almost instinctive, the way someone touches you when they want you to feel safe rather than desired. It reminded him, distantly, of being cared for, of warmth without conditions, of being allowed to rest.

She was new to him, and yet familiar in a way that felt ancient. As if his body recognised her before his mind did. Her presence quieted him. With her, the constant tension he carried seemed to loosen, his thoughts slowing, his breath evening out.

That comfort made her beautiful to him. Not in a loud or dazzling way, but in the way shelter is beautiful when you have been exposed for too long.

It felt like love.

Andy realised he was falling for Charlotte. Properly.

That frightened him.

He reassured himself that everything else was temporary. He would find a job soon. The spending was an investment. He was already convincing enough as a consultant, she would never have to know the truth.

He began applying for jobs on his phone. LinkedIn recommendations. Generic cover letters. One submission after another.

If he could get Charlotte, surely, he could get a job.

When he got home, he lay on his bed and stared at the ceiling.

If Charlotte had invited him to her place, she would expect him to invite her to his.

He looked around his teenage room and knew that could never happen.

The solution formed quickly: borrow an apartment. Rent one. Airbnb.

He wanted to impress her. To show her the life he claimed to live. The lie had grown large enough now that retreat felt impossible.

He sent Charlotte a selfie from the morning.

We look very good together.

She replied instantly, with a heart.

Throughout the day, they messaged about the night, about how nice it had been to wake up together, about how much they already missed each other.

Andy suggested dinner on Saturday. The Grand Hotel. Three Michelin stars.

Wow, that sounds expensive, Charlotte wrote.

My treat, Andy replied.

Okay.

The evening would end at his place.

I'd love to see how you live, she wrote.

Andy didn't hesitate.

During the afternoon, he started booking everything.

The car first.

His mother's company car would have been perfect, but she needed it for a trip out of town. He turned to a car rental site that rented premium cars. The price made him pause, just long enough to feel dizzy, before he tapped confirm.

Then the restaurant.

Three Michelin stars. White tablecloths. Silver cutlery. Staff trained to sense hesitation before it surfaced. Andy told himself it was strategic. An investment. Money had to circulate, didn't it?

Finally, the apartment.

Central. Short-term rental. Exclusive. Panoramic. Floor-to-ceiling windows. Neutral tones. A view that looked staged rather than lived in. He booked two nights, just in case.

He sat on the edge of his bed afterward, phone warm in his hand. The total glared at him from the credit card app.

He closed it.

On Saturday, he packed more clothes than necessary, enough to suggest permanence. He picked up the car from the rental company and drove to the apartment first. He unpacked carefully, placed his three-in-one body wash by the bathtub, arranged objects so that the apartment looked inhabited.

Then he went to pick up Charlotte outside her

building.

She stopped short when she saw the car: black, polished, unmistakable.

"This is... wow," she said, smiling, half-laughing.

Andy shrugged. "I thought we'd make an evening of it."

Inside, the car smelled faintly of leather. Charlotte slid into the passenger seat, smoothing her dress.

He pulled up outside the Grand Hotel, where a valet wordlessly took the keys and drove the car out of sight.

At the Grand Hotel, time seemed to slow.

They were greeted by name. Coats taken smoothly. Charlotte looked around with quiet composure, not needing to prove she belonged.

The menu was heavy. Literally. Andy felt his hand tense as he lifted it.

He ordered confidently. Wine recommended by the sommelier. Dishes that sounded more like short stories than food.

"This feels unreal," Charlotte said softly.

"You get used to it," Andy replied.

The lie landed cleanly.

Dinner unfolded in careful stages, each course arriving like a cue Andy felt expected to respond to correctly.

Charlotte leaned in when Andy spoke, forearms resting lightly against the table, fingers circling the stem of her glass in slow, thoughtful motions. She noticed things, pauses, tone shifts, the way people answered questions instead of what they said.

"This place still feels unreal," she said, glancing around as the waiter cleared their plates. "Like we've stepped into a version of life that assumes everything is already figured out."

Andy smiled.

"You get used to it," he said.

She tilted her head slightly. "Do you? Or do you just learn how to sit comfortably in it?"

The question wasn't accusatory. It was curious.

He hesitated, just long enough to feel exposed. "You learn," he said finally. "How to move through places like this."

Charlotte smiled, but her eyes stayed on him a second longer than necessary. She had noticed the hesitation.

"That sounds tiring," she said gently.

"It can be," Andy replied, then quickly added, "but it's part of the job."

Always the job, he thought. He had built his whole persona around this fictitious job he had. It was the only way he could sound interesting. And interesting was good.

The waiter returned with the next course, plates placed with quiet precision. Charlotte waited until he stepped away before speaking again.

"So," she said, folding her hands together, "tell me something about you that has nothing to do with work."

Andy felt a flicker of panic. His mind went blank in a way that felt almost embarrassing.

What do I do?

"I'm... good at remembering small things," he said after a moment. "Details. Like how people take their coffee. Or which stories they've already told."

Charlotte smiled. "That tells me something."

"Like what?"

"That you are good at paying attention," she said. "And that you're careful with people."

He relaxed slightly.

"But," she continued, not unkindly, "that's not really a hobby."

She took a sip of wine, watching him.

"So what do you do when you're alone?" she asked. "When no one expects anything from you?"

Andy felt the question land deeper than intended.

What do I do?

I lie in bed.

I scroll.

I masturbate.

Nothing much.

He laughed lightly instead. "I used to play Minecraft," he said. "A while ago."

Her eyebrow lifted, attentive. "Used to?"

"Yeah," he said. "I haven't had much time lately."

That wasn't entirely a lie. Time existed. Structure didn't.

"What did you like about playing Minecraft?" she asked.

Andy blinked. No one had ever asked him that.

"I guess..." he said slowly, "I liked building something. Starting with nothing and ending up with a small village or town."

Charlotte nodded, as if that answer mattered more than the game itself.

"That's nice," she said softly. "I used to play Minecraft when I was little. But I like playing Sims instead."

"What about you?" Andy asked, grateful for the shift. "What do you do when you're not... shaping young minds?"

She laughed. "I walk. A lot. It helps me think. And I spend too much time with Sabrina."

"Who's Sabrina?"

"My best friend," Charlotte said. "She knows everything about me."

He smiled. "That sounds... risky."

"It is," she said. "But I trust her."

There was a pause, not empty, but weighted.

Charlotte set her glass down. "You know," she said, lightly but honestly, "you're easier to talk to than I expected."

Andy felt a quiet surge of pride and fear.

"Is that good?" he asked.

"It is," she said.

He laughed, but the sound caught slightly in his chest.

Charlotte smiled.

When the bill arrived, it was placed face down.

Andy handed over his card without looking.

The waiter returned.

"I'm sorry, sir. This card has insufficient funds."

Andy's heart stuttered.

He smiled quickly. "Ah, sorry. I overspent."

He chuckled lightly and handed over another card.

This time, the waiter returned with a nod of approval.

Outside, the night felt cinematic.

"Where to?" Charlotte asked.

"My place?" Andy said.

The apartment glowed when they arrived. Light spilled across polished floors. The city stretched endlessly beyond the windows.

Charlotte moved slowly through the space, fingertips brushing surfaces.

"You live here?" she asked.

"Most of the time," Andy said.

"It's beautiful."

He poured them drinks.

"You are beautiful," he replied.

"Stop it," she said, blushing with embarrassment.

Later, sitting together on the sofa, Charlotte rested her head on his shoulder.

"You spoil me," she said.

Andy felt the familiar hum return, louder

now.

He had crossed something.

This wasn't a story anymore. It was structure. Expectation. Money already spent.

Tomorrow would come, whether he was ready or not.

But tonight, the city glittered beneath borrowed windows, and Andy let himself believe, just a little longer, that this version of him might still hold.

When they finally went to bed, Andy helped her out of her dress, slowly, deliberately. The city shimmered behind her like a distant promise. She turned, kissed him once, lingering.

"Thank you, Andy," she said.

INTERLUDE 3

Charlotte II

Charlotte woke slowly, wrapped in warmth.

Sunday light filtered through the tall windows, pale and unhurried, touching the edges of the room without asking anything of it. For a moment, she stayed still, listening to the city far below, distant enough to feel unreal.

She didn't have to get up.

Still, she slipped quietly out of bed and padded toward the kitchen for a glass of water. The apartment felt cool against her skin. Impersonal. More like a hotel than a home.

Everything was immaculate. Too immaculate. The counters looked as if someone wiped them down daily with deliberate care. Nothing left behind. Nothing forgotten.

She told herself Andy had probably just moved in. Or that, being financially comfortable, he could afford a cleaner.

Men were often like this, she thought: minimalist, practical, uninterested in making a place feel lived in.

She paused in front of a painting on the wall. Neutral. Inoffensive. The kind of art chosen quickly to fill space rather than express anything.

She realised, suddenly, that she didn't have much to point to in her own apartment either. No hobbies, really. Just walking. Long walks that cleared her head. And Sabrina. Coffee, wine, conversations that circled the same questions again and again.

That had always been enough.

People talked so much about passions, about hobbies that defined you. As if not having them meant something was missing. Charlotte had never believed that. Life itself was already full. Work. People. Care. That was where meaning lived for her.

Andy was still asleep when she returned to the bedroom. On his side now, one hand tucked beneath his cheek, his breathing slow and even. In sleep, he looked younger. Less assembled. As if whatever effort he carried during the day loosened its grip at night.

She watched him without hurry.

There was something about Andy that made her feel included. Not impressed. Not dazzled. Included. As if being with him didn't require preparation or performance. She liked that about him. The way he listened. The way he remembered small things. The way his attention felt natural rather than deliberate.

The evening replayed itself in fragments. The

restaurant. The city. His apartment. It had all been beautiful, almost unreal, but what stayed with her wasn't the setting. It was how easily she had laughed. How relaxed she had felt sitting beside him, her head against his shoulder, the world briefly reduced to something manageable.

She slipped back under the covers and moved closer, careful not to wake him. His warmth was immediate, grounding. He stirred slightly, then settled again, his arm finding her waist without opening his eyes.

She smiled.

The thought surprised her, but it didn't feel wrong.

She felt like she was falling in love with Andy.

The word love felt heavy. Serious. It scared her.

What if he doesn't feel the same?

She pushed the thought away almost immediately. Of course, he did. Why wouldn't he? He had been attentive, generous, present. She let herself believe that.

But still, she thought, he does not love me.

Like the loves before, she felt the familiar certainty creep in: Andy would hurt her. Not because he wanted to, but because love, in her experience, always ended that way. With distance. With withdrawal.

And yet, this felt different.

Being with him felt good in a way that unsettled her. Safer. Softer. As if she were standing in a room where the furniture had been rearranged just enough to make space for hope.

Maybe he was not like her ex. The one who had hurt her so deeply that the pain had settled into scars rather than memories. Scars that no longer bled, but still tightened when touched.

She knew those scars well. She carried them carefully.

And still, despite everything she knew, she let herself fall in love, silently. In secret.

His wealth mattered. Not because it impressed her, but because it promised ease. A life without constant calculation. A future where building something: home, family, didn't feel like an uphill struggle.

Charlotte traced absent-minded patterns into the sheet, thinking about how unexpected all of this was. She hadn't planned for anything serious. She hadn't been looking for grand gestures or dramatic beginnings. And yet, here she was, on a Sunday morning, wishing the day would stay exactly as it was.

She wondered what Andy dreamed about. Whether his thoughts followed him into sleep the way hers sometimes did.

He shifted, mumbling something she couldn't quite hear. She leaned in and kissed his shoulder softly, a small reassurance offered without words.

Being here felt easy.

And ease, she knew, was rare.

She closed her eyes and rested against him,

letting the moment exist without questions or demands. Whatever this was, it felt worth staying in a little longer.

For now, that was enough.

Chapter 6

THE GOOD LIFE

Andy and Charlotte slipped into something that looked like a relationship without ever naming it.

They saw each other after work, on weekdays when neither of them had much energy left. Coffee or breakfast before her shifts. Dinner somewhere convenient. Theatre evenings, a shared interest they discovered together. Evenings on the sofa, scrolling separately but touching just enough to stay connected. It felt natural. Earned.

They stayed mostly at Charlotte's place. Whenever Charlotte suggested visiting Andy spontaneously, he met her with excuses: he wasn't home, he was busy, something had come up. There was always a reason.

His car was often "in the workshop," which explained why he seemed to have a different one every now and then. Charlotte accepted it without much thought. The car he liked to rent wasn't always available.

Charlotte talked about the children at the preschool: their small dramas, the way they clung to her legs, the way they cried without embarrassment when something felt unfair. Andy listened, nodding, smiling, storing details. He liked how predictable her days were. How anchored.

He made sure his days sounded similar.

Work was busy. Projects overlapping. Travel maybe, soon. He complained just enough to seem human, never enough to invite concern. Charlotte wasn't suspicious. She trusted him.

Trust was the most expensive thing he had ever been given.

Andy paid for most things.

Not extravagantly, not every time, but often enough to establish a pattern. Dinners. Drinks. Weekend brunches. Theatre tickets. He framed it as obligation, as something a real man did. Charlotte framed it as kindness.

At home, the letters began to pile up.

They arrived quietly, sliding through the mail slot and landing on the hallway floor. Every time Andy came home and saw them, he picked them up quickly, hiding them before his mother could notice.

White envelopes. Logos he recognised immediately. Banks. Credit companies. Services he'd forgotten he'd signed up for.

At first, he stacked them neatly on his desk.

Then he stopped opening them.

Final notice

Reminder

Important information regarding your account

The language shifted before he did.

He kept applying for jobs, but with less urgency. One or two a week. Then one. Then sometimes none.

His mother, tired of watching a third year of unemployment unfold, suggested he apply for government benefits.

That would mean visiting the unemployment agency. Signing in. Proving effort. Searching for jobs every day.

Andy hated the idea. It made him feel small. Reduced. Like a failure.

But he was smart enough to understand that loans needed paying before consequences became irreversible.

He lived two lives in parallel.

One built on lies, dinners, theatre nights, and a woman who believed in him.

The other built on queues, forms, and benefits that disappeared directly into debt.

The money didn't fix anything.

His life grew richer with Charlotte and poorer everywhere else.

After each visit to the agency, his mind blurred the memory. He returned to what felt normal.

One night, during dinner, Andy took a photo of Charlotte and posted it on Instagram.

My everything

It caught the attention of Tommy, his old high-school best friend. They hadn't really spoken since university.

Tommy messaged him, asking about the girlfriend, suggesting they grab a beer, like old times.

They met at the same bar they used to go to after high school. Cheap beer. A mix of students, academics, alcoholics, working people, and men with nowhere else to be.

Tommy looked the same in a way Andy found unsettling. Older, but settled. A regular job. Complaints that were small and specific.

"So," Andy said, leaning back. "What are you up to these days?"

"Accounting," Tommy said. "Small firm."

"That's good."

"Good is relative," Tommy shrugged. "Didn't really need an MBA for it. Feels like being a barista with a degree. But the job market's insane. When they offered, I took it."

"The job market's crazy," Andy agreed. "Makes no sense."

"Exactly," Tommy replied. "Everyone's unemployed, markets are booming, and nobody wants to admit how fucked we are."

Andy liked hearing it. It felt like old times. Like honesty was still possible.

When the conversation turned to him, Andy didn't hesitate.

Consulting. Finance. PCP. International clients. Long hours. Good money.

"Wow," Tommy said. "I'm glad it worked out for you. And who's the girl?"

Andy talked about Charlotte. Her beauty. Her warmth. How lucky he was.

Tommy nodded, impressed. Maybe a little envious.

Andy felt a sting of guilt, but also relief. Lying was easier than honesty. Made him look like he was a couple of steps ahead. Honesty required context. Explanation. Shame.

They hugged goodbye outside the bar. Promised to keep in touch.

They didn't.

December arrived quietly.

Charlotte talked about Christmas early. Her parents. Traditions. Familiar arguments. Comfort.

They decided to spend the holidays apart. It made sense. It was still early.

"Next year," Charlotte said casually one evening, brushing her teeth. "We could do something together."

Andy smiled at her reflection.

"Yeah," he said. "Next year."

At home, his mother decorated quietly. The same ornaments as always. Preparing for his uncle's visit and his new Thai wife.

She noticed Andy was rarely home and finally asked if he had met someone.

Embarrassed, he answered like a teenager:

"Yes, Mum. I have a girlfriend."

Her face lit up. "Oh, Andy! What's her name?"

"Charlotte."

"What a beautiful name. When will I meet her?"

"Someday."

Probably never.

On Christmas Eve, Andy sat on his bed, surrounded by unopened letters, scrolling through photos Charlotte sent from her parents 'house. Candles. Food. Smiling faces.

She looked happy.

They exchanged hearts. Jokes. Small affirmations.

Andy felt loved.

He also felt trapped.

That night, lying awake in his teenage bed, the poster on the wall curling slightly more each year, he counted numbers instead of sheep. Balances. Due dates. Limits already reached.

He told himself January would reset everything. New year. New chances.

Outside, the city was quiet. Inside, the room felt smaller than ever.

Somewhere else, Charlotte was asleep in a familiar bed, dreaming of a future that still felt possible.

Andy closed his eyes and held onto that thought as long as he could.

Chapter 7

THE NEW YEAR

The airport was buzzing with life, the steady heartbeat of the world moving people towards departures and reunions. Andy stood by arrivals with a bouquet of flowers, watching the screens change.

As he waited for Charlotte's flight from her parents 'place, he imagined taking her somewhere far away. White beaches. Palm trees. A place where she would glow effortlessly, untouched by winter or worry.

That evening, they were meant to celebrate New Year's Eve at her friend's apartment, then stay over at his rented place. His anxiety sat high in his chest, not only because the Airbnb was painfully expensive, but because he would meet her friends. Lying to Charlotte had become second nature. Lying to her friends felt like crossing another line.

The lie had escalated.

He felt buried by debt, weighed down and unseen.

Then he saw her.

Charlotte stepped out through the sliding doors, her face lighting up the moment she spotted him. Absence had sharpened something between them. Made it stick.

"Oh Andy, you didn't have to," she said, taking the flowers and smelling them. "They're beautiful."

They walked to the car together.

"You finally got your car back," she said lightly. "Maybe you should get a new one. This one's always breaking down."

Andy nodded, smiling faintly. The comment felt strangely domestic.

"I'm so excited for you to meet my friends," she continued. "Especially Sabrina. You're going to love her."

Andy focused on navigating out of the parking lot.

She interpreted his silence as calm confidence. It made him more attractive to her.

She felt a familiar intensity rise in her, a physical certainty she recognised without thinking. Her body was ahead of her again, tuned to that quiet, monthly insistence that made closeness feel necessary rather than optional.

"Are we going to your place?" she asked.

"Yes," Andy said.

"Good."

Back at the apartment, Charlotte quickly arranged the flowers in a vase. Without warning, she crossed the room and kissed him passionately, pulling him with her toward the bedroom. Whatever urgency had built during their time apart spilled over quickly.

She pushed Andy back onto the bed, laughing breathlessly, momentum carrying them both. Her top came away quickly, discarded somewhere on the floor, the moment unfolding faster than thought, faster than hesitation.

Her breasts, perfect and sweet like two pears, reflected in the daylight.

Andy barely had time to catch up. They kissed with a hunger that felt pent-up, overdue, as if something long restrained had finally broken loose.

There was no careful choreography this time, no pauses to negotiate the moment. Just bodies finding each other with instinctive certainty.

She was on top.

She rode with confidence, urgency, her movements decisive and unguarded. Andy followed her rhythm, caught up in it, the room narrowing to breath, touch, heat.

It built quickly, overwhelmingly, like music reaching its final movement all at once. No preparation. No distance. No reflection. No protection.

Only release.

Afterward, they lay tangled together, the air still heavy, the moment already slipping into memory. Intense. Unexamined. Irreversible.

She placed a hand over her stomach without quite realising she was doing it, lingering there for half a second too long.

"Look at the time," she said softly, exhaling. "We should get ready for the party."

As evening settled in, Andy put on a dark suit. Charlotte wore a red dress that caught the light. Together, they went to Sabrina's apartment.

The place was crowded and warm. Music played too loudly. Coats and shoes were scattered everywhere. Someone insisted on calling cheap sparkling wine champagne. Someone else kept reminding everyone theirs was better.

Sabrina appeared out of nowhere.

"Charlotte! What a lovely dress!" she exclaimed, kissing her cheek, then turning to Andy with a grin. "And you must be Andy. The famous finance guy."

Andy laughed. "Famous already? That was fast."

"Word spreads fast around town," Sabrina said. "I also saw you two went to the theatre some weeks ago."

"Yes," Charlotte said. "We saw this play called Miss Julie."

"Ohhh," Sabrina said, theatrically. "It's good. Did you like it?"

"We did," Charlotte said. "I tried to get Andy to do some role-playing inspired by it afterward."

Andy groaned. "That is not true."

"It absolutely is," Charlotte said. "He refused."

Sabrina laughed. "You didn't?"

"I did," Charlotte said.

"Anyway, I'll come kidnap you later. I promised three people I'd say hello and I'm already late."

"Go," Charlotte said. "We'll still be here."

Sabrina winked at Andy. "Behave."

"I'll try," he said.

As Sabrina disappeared into the crowd, Charlotte turned to Andy, smiling. "She's great, right?"

Andy nodded. "I like her."

Charlotte smiled.

They moved through the room as Charlotte greeting familiar faces. Andy stayed close to Charlotte, his hand resting lightly at her waist. No one questioned him. Being the finance guy was explanation enough.

As midnight approached, the room tightened with anticipation. Phones were raised. Voices joined in uneven countdowns.

Ten.

Nine.

Eight.

Charlotte turned toward Andy, her face bright with wine and excitement.

Three.

Two.

One.

The room erupted.

Should auld acquaintance be forgot,
And never brought to mind?

Andy kissed her.

It wasn't careful. It wasn't polite. It was full

and immediate, the kind of kiss that dissolved context.

Should auld acquaintance be forgot,
And auld lang syne?

"I love you," Charlotte said into his mouth.

For auld lang syne, my dear,
For auld lang syne,
We'll tak a cup o'kindness yet,
For auld lang syne

The words escaped before she could stop them.

She froze.

"Oh..." she said, pulling back. "I didn't..."

Her face flushed. Panic overtook embarrassment. She turned and pushed through the crowd toward the bathroom.

Andy followed.

He knocked gently.

"Charlotte?"

Silence.

Then a breath, sharp and uneven.

"I'm so stupid," she said through the door.

"You're not," Andy replied. "Please. Let me in."

The lock clicked.

She stood by the sink, mascara smudged beneath her eyes, arms folded tightly against herself.

"I didn't mean to," she said quickly. "I just..."

Andy stepped closer.

"You just what?"

She laughed once, brittle. "I love you. There. I said it. Now you can leave."

Andy took her by the waist and kissed her. Not to silence her, just to ground her.

"I love you too," he said.

The words surprised him with their weight.

Charlotte searched his face. Found no hesitation.

"Oh," she said softly.

Relief broke through. She laughed, wiped at her cheeks.

"I made such a big deal out of it," she said. "I'm sorry."

"You didn't," Andy said.

She leaned into him.

"I've been disappointed so many times," she said quietly. "I don't want that again."

"You won't," Andy said.

"Promise?"

He met her gaze.

"I promise."

When they returned to the party, nothing had changed. Music played. Glasses clinked. Time moved on.

But something between them had settled into place.

They woke up together on New Year's Day in the rented apartment: bodies warm and familiar.

For brunch, they went to the Bucharest Café. The city felt slower, as if it were recovering collectively. The café felt timeless: high ceilings, mirrors, marble tables.

Andy ordered confidently.

"You're not even hungover," Charlotte teased.

"Professional stamina," he said.

She laughed.

"I'm sorry about last night," she said suddenly. "I felt silly."

"You didn't," Andy said, taking her hand. "I'm still here."

She looked at him.

"I love you," he said.

"I love you too."

When the bill arrived, Andy reached for it.

His card declined.

He tried another.

Declined.

Andy smiled too quickly. "Sorry. My funds are in Zürich. Tax reasons. They're being transferred... tomorrow"

Charlotte didn't question it. She simply reached for the bill.

"I've got it," she said.

He protested weakly

"I want to," she said. "Let me spoil you."

Andy nodded.

He felt grateful. Relieved. And faintly hollow.

As they left, Charlotte slipped her hand into his.

"Happy New Year," she said.

Andy smiled back.

It was the first day of the year.

And for the first time, the future felt real enough to be frightening.

INTERLUDE 4

Charlotte III

Charlotte thought about the party more than she wanted to.

Not in sharp images, but in sensations: the noise, the closeness, the way the room had pressed in on her just before midnight. The warmth of the wine. The uneven countdown echoing through the apartment. The kiss that hadn't been careful enough.

And the words.

She hadn't planned to say them. She knew that now. They had slipped out, carried by the moment, by her body, by something deeper she hadn't fully controlled. She could admit that to herself calmly, without embarrassment.

She wasn't ashamed of loving him.

What unsettled her was how easily she had needed to say it. As if the words had been waiting for an opening. As if they had wanted to escape her mouth, tumbling out clumsily, like alphabet pasta spilling from a child's bowl.

It wasn't the first time she had been in love.

In high school, she had been with a boy for years. Her first real relationship. Her first real love. She had fallen deeply, quietly, completely. She never told him she loved him, not because she didn't feel it, but because she assumed it was obvious.

That love, once established, didn't need announcing.

She built her life around him without noticing she was doing it. Learned his routines. Became close to his sisters. His parents. His relatives. She belonged there. Or so she thought.

On graduation day, he told her it was over.

Just like that.

The memory still arrived without warning. The way the ground had seemed to drop beneath her, the future collapsing inward, crushing itself into something unrecognisable. Everything she had invested: time, trust, identity, had been quietly dismantled.

After that, love had felt dangerous.

She learned to be careful. To wait. To measure. To never give someone everything before knowing they would stay.

And then came Andy.

She knew why she had said what she said at the party.

She recognised the feeling, those days when emotions rose faster, when closeness felt urgent, almost necessary.

When desire and attachment blurred into something louder than thought. It didn't excuse her behaviour, but it explained it.

Still.

What surprised her most wasn't what she'd done, but how quickly everything had moved on afterward.

Andy had followed her. He'd said the right words. He'd kissed her. He'd told her he loved her too. And then, just like that. Filed away. No questions. No daylight conversation. No return to it once the music stopped.

Part of her had expected more.

Not drama. Not reassurance. Just curiosity. A moment where they might sit with it together. Where he might ask why it had mattered so much to her. Where she could tell him about the girl she used to be and the heartbreak she still carried quietly.

She wanted him to want to know her there.

Instead, Andy smiled. Held her hand. Took her for brunch. Loved her in gestures, if not in words.

Sometimes she grew quiet, and Andy would ask if everything was okay. She answered automatically:

"I'm fine," and the day continued.

Inside, her thoughts tangled. Over-analysing small moments. Replaying conversations. Searching for meaning where none had been offered.

She reassured herself that this was normal. That it was enough.

Maybe this was how Andy handled things, by

smoothing them over, by moving forward instead of digging. Maybe depth, for him, was something private, something handled internally.

She noticed how little he spoke about his childhood. About his parents 'divorce. As if those things had been absorbed and flattened by time, stored somewhere unreachable.

Still, a small disappointment settled beneath her ribs.

She wanted him to ask how she had felt.

She wanted him to wonder why she had cried.

She wanted to be known there, not simply forgiven.

She scolded herself for wanting more. For making something heavy out of something good. People expressed care differently. Men especially. She knew that. She taught children every day not to demand answers before others were ready.

Andy hadn't pulled away. He hadn't punished her vulnerability. He had stayed.

That mattered.

But there was something else.

His calm felt distant. His lack of questions felt like disengagement. Not cruelty, but absence.

For now, she chose to let it rest.

But sometimes, lying awake later, she replayed the moment, not the kiss, not the words, but the silence afterward. The way he hadn't looked back, hadn't asked, hadn't stayed with it.

And she wondered, quietly, whether love that moved on so easily could also disappear the same way.

She hoped not.
She didn't want to lose this.
Not now.
Never.

Chapter 8

THE RELATIONSHIP

The new year began like a new chapter in life. A fresh start. Or at least the promise of one.

Andy and Charlotte woke up together more often now, their days shaped by shared routines rather than plans. Mornings blurred into each other coffee, brushing teeth, quiet jokes exchanged half-awake.

They said I love you easily.

Sometimes it slipped out absent-mindedly, while buttoning coats or searching for keys. Sometimes it was deliberate, held for a moment longer, as if to test whether it still fit. Andy felt a strange mix of relief and unease every time he said it.

The words were true.

He was not.

That was the problem.

The lie was eating at him. Not sharply, not all at once, but steadily. The relationship felt real, warm, meaningful. And yet it rested on something hollow.

Andy wasn't cruel. He wasn't calculating. He hadn't planned to deceive anyone. He had wanted to be impressive. Wanted to be seen as capable, successful, worth choosing.

Society and social media had taught him what that looked like. When he couldn't meet the standard, he adjusted the story.

What he hadn't anticipated was how far the adjustment would go.

Sitting beside the woman he loved, lying about his job, his money, his stability, it felt like a slow internal bleeding. A private kind of violence. He slept, but poorly. Alone, he barely slept at all.

Guilt became constant.

Charlotte, meanwhile, was happy.

She trusted him completely. She felt balanced, grounded, certain. Andy gave her a sense of direction. Being with him felt like moving forward.

Andy felt the same, only when he was with her.

Alone, panic returned.

Someday the truth would come out.

She would understand. Wouldn't she?

That day felt far away. Distant enough to ignore.

He still had time. Time to find a job. Time to make the lie obsolete. Time to become the man he claimed to be before anyone noticed the difference.

Charlotte wanted to talk.

Not casually, deeply.

She wanted to understand him. His childhood. His family. How he became who he was. She wanted vulnerability exchanged evenly. The scene on New Year's Eve still sat with her, unexamined. She wanted to explain herself, her fear, her past heartbreak, and she wanted Andy to meet her there.

Andy resisted without meaning to.

Not because he was guarding a lie, but because he had learned to guard himself.

Men didn't talk about feelings. Men handled things. Men provided. Men stayed steady. That was the model he had absorbed early and never questioned.

Emotion was indulgence. Vulnerability was weakness. And weakness was dangerous.

Showing emotion and vulnerability was femininity. He did not perceive himself as a female.

Charlotte noticed the resistance, not as suspicion, but as absence.

She adjusted her approach, asking questions the way she spoke to children at work: gently, patiently, assuming there was something worth uncovering beneath the surface.

"How are you really?"

"What worries you?"

"What do you want things to look like in a few years?"

Andy answered, but never fully.

He spoke in generalities. Ambition. Stability. Stress at work. He stayed close to the truth without touching it.

Charlotte felt it.

Not as deception, just as distance.

Andy, meanwhile, carried his real conversations silently.

With banking apps.

With unopened letters.

With credit limits stretched thin.

With buy-now-pay-later schemes quietly demanding attention.

Guilt became a low, constant hum.

At night, Charlotte rested her head on his chest and spoke about the future with certainty. Apartments. Space. Light. A place that felt like home. She teased the bland artwork in his apartment and laughed about how "temporary" it felt.

Andy smiled. They weren't his artwork.

Inside, he calculated.

Rent. Deposits. Furniture. The cost of a life he couldn't afford.

"Not now," Charlotte said one evening. "But soon. When it feels right."

"It already feels right," Andy said and meant it.

She grinned. "Rents are insane though. For a bigger apartment. What if the housing market crashes?"

"Yeah," Andy said.

"Then we could even buy!" she laughed.

"That's something old people do."

To Charlotte, money felt manageable. Solvable. Something they would figure out together.

Andy listened, heart full and stomach tight.

At home, the letters waited.

He hid them less carefully now, stuffed into drawers, pushed behind books, buried under things he no longer used.

Some nights, he lay awake beside Charlotte, rehearsing confessions that ended in forgiveness. Other nights, he convinced himself there was still time.

He could say he'd been laid off. Everyone was being laid off. The job market was brutal.

But then what?

Then he wouldn't be a provider. Wouldn't be steady. Wouldn't be what he thought she needed.

January stretched on.

Andy applied for jobs obsessively. Interviews appeared, then vanished. Tests drained him. Logic puzzles. Personality screens. Endless assessments that led nowhere.

Andy and Charlotte were building something.

That was the terrifying part.

Love was no longer a feeling. It was a direction. And Andy was walking forward carrying a secret that grew heavier with every step.

One evening, he came home to find his mother sitting quietly at the kitchen table.

Two envelopes lay in front of her.

She didn't look angry.

She looked disappointed. Worried.

"Andy," she said, tapping the letters. "Can you explain this?"

Chapter 9

THE COUNSEL

Andy stood in the doorway for a moment longer than necessary. His mother sat at the kitchen table with two envelopes laid neatly in front of her, aligned with the edge, as if order might help. She had not opened them. She did not need to.

"Sit down," she said.

Andy did.

The silence between them was familiar. Heavy. Careful. The kind that had replaced shouting years ago.

"These came this morning," she said, tapping the envelopes with one finger. "They are not the first."

Andy nodded.

She waited.

He did not speak.

"Andy," she said finally, softer now. "I need you to explain."

He looked at the table. At the small scratch

near the edge, he had made as a teenager. At his hands, folded too tightly together.

"I did not mean for it to get like this," he said.

She did not interrupt.

"I thought it would be temporary. Just... until I got back on my feet."

"Temporary what?" she asked.

He swallowed.

"Well... temporary," he said. "I am unemployed, living at my mother's place. I want to live a life, not feel like an adolescent."

"And you thought it would be smart to take out credit card loans and bury yourself in buy-now-pay-later invoices?" she asked.

He sat there quietly.

"Just so you can live?" she continued. "I do not understand this, Andy. What is this talk about temporary? What exactly is temporary?"

"The spending," he said. "The cards. The pretending."

That made her look up.

"Pretending?"

Andy exhaled, long and uneven.

For a moment, he considered standing up, walking out, not saying another word. But he knew he couldn't.

"I told my new girlfriend, Charlotte, that I work in consulting," he said. "That I am doing well. Better than I am."

His mother closed her eyes briefly. Not in anger. In disappointment.

"How long?" she asked.

Andy stayed silent.

"How long?" she said again, louder this time.

"Since the beginning."

She did not raise her voice again.

"Why?"

Andy hesitated, then said it all at once, afraid that if he paused, he would not finish.

"Because I didn't want her to see me like this. Because I wanted to be impressive. Because everyone expects you to have your life together at my age. Because I wanted to be with someone. Because I didn't want her to leave."

His voice cracked on the last word.

"I love her," he said. "I really do. I have never felt like this about anyone."

It felt humiliating to confess this to his mother. But there was no other place for it to go.

She studied him carefully now, the way she used to when he came home late as a teenager, eyes too bright, explanations rehearsed.

"You thought money would make you worth staying for?" she asked.

Andy nodded.

She leaned back in her chair, folding her arms, not defensively, but to hold herself together.

"You know I understand pressure," she said. "I understand wanting to look like you are coping."

"I just need time," Andy said. "Once I get a job, it will all disappear. The lie won't matter anymore."

His mother shook her head slowly.

"That is not how lies work," she said. "They do not disappear. They wait."

Andy stared at the floor.

"What am I supposed to do?" he asked. "Tell her now? Destroy everything?"

She thought for a moment.

"Andy," she said carefully, "what you are afraid of losing, you are already risking by not telling her."

He looked up at her then, eyes wide, almost childlike.

"If she loves you," his mother continued, "she doesn't love you because you buy her dinners. She loves you because she thinks she knows you."

"I haven't only bought dinners," Andy said. "I've rented luxury cars. Short-term apartments. I've splurged on gifts. Just so she doesn't see this living hell I'm actually in."

His mother sat quietly, looking at him.

"The worst part," Andy added, a tear running down his cheek, "is that she trusts me."

"She trusts you," she repeated.

"I don't want to hurt her," he said.

"I know," she replied. "But you already are. Just quietly."

The words landed hard.

She softened again.

"This mess..." she gestured at the envelopes "...we can work through. Budgets. Payment plans. That's solvable." She paused. "How much are we talking about?"

"More than thirty thousand dollars," he said, breaking.

His mother closed her eyes.

"That is a lot," she said quietly. "You do not have that kind of money."

Andy felt his body sink.

"But Charlotte is not a practical problem," she continued. "She is a person. And people deserve the truth before they build their lives around a story."

Andy pressed his palms together, fighting the urge to argue.

"What if she leaves me?" he asked.

His mother did not answer immediately.

"Then she leaves," she said finally. "And that will hurt. But it will hurt less than watching this grow until it collapses on both of you."

He nodded slowly.

"She will think I am pathetic," he said.

"She might be angry," his mother replied. "She might be disappointed. But if she loves you, she will want to know who you are when things are difficult, not just when they look good."

Andy felt the familiar hum rise again, louder now.

"You raised me to do better than this," he said quietly.

She reached across the table and placed her hand over his.

"I raised you to tell the truth when it mattered," she said. "This is one of those times."

He sat there for a long moment, absorbing it.

"I don't know how to say it," he said.

"Start with I was scared," she replied. "And don't try to fix it in the same sentence."

Andy nodded.

The envelopes stayed on the table between them.

Nothing had been resolved.

But for the first time in months, something had been named.

Chapter 10

THE KANGAROOS

Andy and Charlotte decided to have a date at the city zoo.

They had both been there often as children. On school trips. With parents. On weekends that smelled of popcorn and wet coats. They liked to joke that they might have crossed paths once— passed each other on the playground, stood in the same line for ice cream— without ever knowing.

If they had, neither of them remembered.

The zoo was crowded that weekend in a familiar way: families drifting slowly between enclosures, children tugging at sleeves, the air filled with popcorn, damp wool, and the distant calls of animals answering one another.

Andy and Charlotte walked side by side, her arm hooked casually through his.

It had been Charlotte's idea.

"I haven't been here since I was a kid," she had said that morning, smiling into her coffee. "And I just want to do something… normal."

Andy had agreed too quickly.

Normal sounded safe.

They passed flamingos standing impossibly still, balanced like ornaments, and monkeys shrieking and leaping with theatrical urgency. Charlotte laughed easily, pointing things out, narrating facts she half-remembered from childhood visits.

Andy watched her more than the animals.

He had decided. Carefully. Deliberately.

Today would be the day.

The words were ready. He had rehearsed them on the bus, on the walk there, in the quiet gaps between Charlotte's sentences.

I need to tell you something.

I've been scared.

I didn't mean for it to go this far.

Every version ended the same way in his head: silence, then questions, then a future he could not predict.

They stopped by the giraffes. Charlotte tilted her head back, shading her eyes.

"Imagine being that tall," she said. "You'd see everything coming."

Andy smiled, distracted.

"There's something I want to talk to you about," he said.

She didn't hear him. A baby giraffe had stepped into view, wobbling slightly on its legs.

"Oh, look," she said softly. "How cute. A little giraffe."

Andy hesitated. Maybe this wasn't the moment. But he had promised himself.

Telling her in a public space felt safer somehow. Less dramatic. Maybe emotions wouldn't take over. Maybe logic would prevail.

They walked on, down a narrow path shaded by palm trees hanging low overhead.

"Cozy," Charlotte commented.

Andy nodded.

"Charlotte," he began again. "There's something I want to talk to you about."

She turned toward him immediately, attentive. Open.

Her blue eyes held warmth and care.

"Yes?" she said with excitement.

The word landed gently. Patiently.

Andy opened his mouth...

...and a child screamed nearby as a peacock suddenly spread its feathers across the path, brilliant and loud.

Phones rose instantly. A small crowd gathered.

"Oh my god, look at that," Charlotte laughed, already moving toward it.

The moment slipped away.

Andy told himself it was fine. There would be another opening. A quieter bench. Coffee later. He didn't want to drop something heavy in the middle of a crowd anyway.

They reached the kangaroo enclosure not long after.

Charlotte stopped short.

"Oh," she said, smiling. "Kangaroos."

Warmth moved through Andy's chest.

"Kangaroos," she repeated, amused. "Do you remember the first thing you ever asked me?"

He did.

"Yes," he said, chuckling. "Do you like kangaroos?"

She laughed.

"I thought you were insane," she said. "Why kangaroos?"

"I honestly don't know," he admitted. "I was this close to unsending it."

"But you didn't," she said.

"And you replied."

"I did," she said, looking down, kicking at the gravel. "Because it was harmless. Fun."

She leaned against the railing, watching the animals move lazily in the sun. One kangaroo scratched its chest, completely unbothered, indifferent to being observed.

"I like that about you," Charlotte added. "You didn't try too hard."

Andy stepped behind her and wrapped his arms around her. She leaned into him, fitting easily.

Nostalgia arrived quietly. The excitement of those first messages, the simplicity of expecting nothing.

Truth hovered, then retreated.

She turned within his arms.

"Andy," she said softly. "Was there something

you wanted to talk to me about?"

His stomach tightened.

Now.

"Yes," he said. "I've been..."

She watched him closely, sensing the weight of it, encouraging without pressure. This felt like the moment she'd been waiting for. Proof that he was opening up.

"You know what," he said instead, smiling. "It's nothing. I just wanted to say how beautiful you are today. And how much I appreciate you."

She smiled immediately.

"I love you," she said.

They kissed.

If he told her now, it would contaminate the moment.

The warmth of the day.

The ease of her laughter.

The simplicity of us.

He stayed quiet, holding her a little longer.

"What are you thinking about?" Charlotte asked gently.

"I'm enjoying this," he said, kissing her forehead, eyes on the kangaroos hopping awkwardly across the enclosure.

She smiled, satisfied. She felt this was a beginning. The first step toward him opening up.

They finished the zoo slowly. Ice cream. A gift shop, where they bought a small stuffed kangaroo as a souvenir. A tired, contented silence on the way home.

By the time they parted that evening, the decision had settled inside him.

Not now.

Not today.

He would tell her when there was something to tell. When the truth had softened. When the lie had dissolved into irrelevance.

Maybe his mother was wrong. She had made her own mistakes.

That morning, before they left for the zoo, Andy had applied for a position at PCP.

Perspective Capital Partners.

The application had gone through smoothly. No errors. No immediate rejection. He had even received a confirmation email that sounded promising.

We will be in touch.

It felt like a sign.

Hope.

On the way home, he reread the email, letting hope do what it always did, expand quickly, without evidence.

This would fix it.

He would get the job.

The money would come.

The story would align with reality.

By the time the truth mattered, it wouldn't be a lie anymore.

Andy watched Charlotte disappear down the street, feeling both lighter and heavier at the same time.

He told himself he had made the right choice.

The kangaroos had looked peaceful.

Unbothered by what waited beyond the fence.

Andy wished, briefly, that he could be like that.

Then he put his phone back in his pocket and went home, already rehearsing the man he hoped to become.

Chapter 11

THE FLOWERS

Charlotte kept thinking about the zoo. Not the animals themselves, but the moment by the kangaroos. The pause. The hesitation in Andy's voice. The way he had almost said something and then chosen another path instead.

She replayed it not as disappointment, but as progress.

He had been close to opening up. She felt certain of that. Over time, she had learned to recognise when someone was standing at the edge of themselves. Andy wasn't closed, he was careful. Protective.

What Charlotte didn't know was that he had been about to confess.

Still, she believed something deep had almost surfaced. That alone made her feel closer to him.

In the days that followed, she noticed small things more keenly. The way he remembered details about her work. How he listened without interrupting. How he held her when she grew quiet, not demanding explanations, just being there.

She felt loved.

And she wanted to give something back, not dramatically, not to prove anything. Just a gesture. Something simple and unexpected.

Valentine's Day was approaching.

The idea came to her one afternoon while folding laundry, moving slowly through her apartment, enjoying the quiet.

Flowers. At his office. On Valentine's Day. Simple. Sweet.

And since she had the day off, she would be the courier herself. That felt more personal. More real.

She imagined Andy in the middle of his workday: surprised, smiling, maybe a little embarrassed.

She chose the bouquet carefully. Nothing extravagant. Clean colours. A few roses. Enough to suggest love and continuity. Warm tones. Something sincere rather than showy.

On Valentine's Day morning, she checked the address again.

Perspective Capital Partners. PCP.

A glass building. Central. Impressive without being ostentatious.

As she walked toward the florist to collect the bouquet she'd pre-ordered, she thought about Andy's reaction.

Will he be happy? Of course.

Surprised? Definitely.

Then another thought arrived, unexpected.

What if I surprise him properly?

She stopped in front of a shop window and caught her reflection. Ordinary. Sweet. Practical.

She glanced down, suddenly aware of what she was wearing underneath.

Boring underwear.

She turned around immediately and walked home.

If she was going to do this, she would do it properly.

Back in her apartment, she stripped quickly and searched for her red lingerie. She hadn't worn it in a long time. When she found it, it still fit, mostly. The bra was a little tight, but she decided to endure it.

Andy would like it.

She adjusted her hair, her makeup, nothing dramatic, just enough to feel intentional, then got dressed again.

Flowers first. Then PCP.

As Andy sat at the unemployment agency filling out forms and submitting applications, Charlotte stepped into the lobby of Perspective Capital Partners.

The space was exactly what she had imagined: bright, minimal, calm in a way that suggested efficiency. People moved with purpose, coats over arms, phones pressed to ears.

The receptionist barely looked up.

"Yes?"

"I'm here to leave flowers for Andy Matthew-man," Charlotte said, smiling. "Consulting."

The receptionist turned to her screen and began typing.

Paused.

Typed again.

"Can you spell the name?" she asked flatly. "Matthew-man? As in Matthew man?"

"Yes," Charlotte said. "Matthewman."

The receptionist scrolled, clicked, frowned.

"There's no one by that name here," she said.

Charlotte blinked. "Maybe under a different department?"

Another click. A sigh, exaggerated, impatient.

"No," the receptionist said. "No Andy Matthewman here."

Charlotte felt a brief flush of embarrassment, not fear, just that familiar social heat of having misjudged something.

Her bra was digging in painfully, but she ignored it.

"Could you maybe check a bit more?" Charlotte asked gently. "I'm here to surprise him for Valentine's Day."

She smiled. The receptionist rolled her eyes.

"Nope," she said. "Can't find him."

Then she hesitated.

"You know what," the receptionist added, softening slightly, "it could be that he's new. Or from a subsidiary. Sometimes they're not listed yet."

"Yes," Charlotte said quickly, relieved.

"I'd need time to track him down," the receptionist said. "But I can take the flowers and make sure he gets them."

Disappointed, Charlotte nodded. "Okay."

The receptionist pulled out a pen and paper.

"Write his name," she said. "I'll pass them on."

Charlotte wrote Andy Matthewman carefully and placed the bouquet on the counter.

The tight bra suddenly felt like a pointless sacrifice.

Outside, the city reclaimed her immediately, traffic, voices, movement.

She walked away smiling, though a little deflated. It hadn't gone as planned. She hadn't seen his office. Hadn't surprised him in person.

She wondered briefly what his workspace looked like.

Minimal?

Neat?

Messy?

She would never know.

Andy had mentioned international offices, affiliates, temporary arrangements. Companies were large. Systems imperfect.

She trusted him.

Even if the delivery hadn't been perfect, the intention mattered. She imagined his reaction later: the smile, the teasing, the warmth.

That evening they were meeting at the Grand Hotel for a romantic Valentine's dinner.

That, at least, she was looking forward to.

And to Andy's smile when he realised someone had been thinking of him all day.

Chapter 12

THE VALENTINE'S DAY

Andy continued deeper into his rabbit hole of loans and credit, convincing himself that this, this performance, was necessary. That he had to show Charlotte that he was someone stable, impressive, worth choosing.

He decided to treat her to a Valentine's Day dinner at the Grand Hotel.

To impress her.

To remind her of the first time.

The zoo had filled them with nostalgia, warmed something old and hopeful. He wanted to recreate that feeling. Preserve it.

The lie? Yes. He would tell her the truth, eventually. But his application to PCP was progressing. He was even going in for an interview soon. That changed things. That meant the truth could wait. Or better yet, that the lie might simply dissolve once reality caught up.

They agreed to meet at the Grand Hotel bar before dinner.

Andy arrived early and ordered whisky sours for both of them, paying with his Amex card, flashy, heavy, almost reassuring in his hand, racking up credit like a rabbit cornered by adrenaline.

The Grand Hotel looked the same as it always did.

Warm light spilling through tall windows. Staff moving in smooth, choreographed silence. Everything designed to feel permanent, as if the building itself had never doubted its place in the world.

Charlotte arrived, her coat taken immediately by a man who looked like he'd been trained never to hesitate. She scanned the room, eyes already searching for Andy.

She was excited. Nervous. Curious.

Andy waved her over.

She walked toward him, beautiful in a way that felt effortless. Her blue eyes said more than words ever could.

"You look beautiful," Andy said, emotion rising unexpectedly in his throat. He kissed her cheek. "I ordered us whisky sours."

"Oh, how gentlemanly," she smiled, taking a sip.

Andy relaxed a little.

"Did you get any surprises today?" Charlotte

asked casually, but not carelessly.

"Surprises?" Andy repeated, buying himself time. "Well, yeah. A client closed his account."

Charlotte placed a hand on his shoulder immediately.

"Oh, sweetheart," she said. "There will always be new clients. You're the best." She hesitated. "No... other surprises?"

"Nope," Andy said too quickly. "Just that."

They were shown to their table.

Charlotte glanced around, recognition flickering across her face.

"Do you remember last time we were here?" she asked.

Andy smiled. "Of course."

Their first extravagant date. Three Michelin stars. The feeling of stepping into a version of life that felt cinematic, unreal. Back then, everything had still been possibility.

They ordered champagne. A set menu. Andy handled it with practised ease.

Tonight, Charlotte wasn't looking for extravagance.

She was looking for acknowledgment.

"Did you have a good day?" she asked.

"Yeah," Andy replied. "Busy."

She nodded, waiting.

"How was work?" she asked gently.

"Busy," he repeated. "This project's taking most of my time."

"What kind of project?" she asked.

Andy stiffened.

"Well... it's a client merging investments into one basket," he said vaguely, then cut himself off. "You probably wouldn't understand."

The first course arrived.

They ate quietly.

"I went into the city today," Charlotte said after a moment.

"Oh yeah?" Andy replied, focused on the plate.

"Mm. Had the day off."

"That's nice," he said. "You deserve it."

He didn't ask what she'd done.

Inside her, something tightened.

"I was thinking about the zoo," she tried again. "The kangaroos."

Andy laughed. "Still obsessed?"

"A little," she smiled.

She waited for something, anything, that showed he'd noticed. That he'd seen the effort. The intention.

Nothing came.

As the courses passed, Charlotte felt a familiar ache rise: the quiet disappointment of wanting to be seen without having to ask.

She told herself Andy wasn't careless. Just inattentive. Some people didn't register gestures unless they were spelled out.

It didn't mean anything.

Still, she tried once more.

"What did you get up to today, really?" she asked lightly.

Her thoughts scattered. Had the receptionist forgotten? Had Andy received the flowers and dismissed them? Had something gone wrong?

No. She stopped herself. Don't spiral.

"Just a normal day," Andy said.

Normal.

The word landed heavier than he intended.

Charlotte nodded and took a sip of champagne, letting the bubbles distract her. She didn't want to ruin the evening. Didn't want Valentine's Day to turn into expectations.

Andy felt the pressure shift.

Something was wrong. The easiest solution would be to ask. But asking might rupture the evening. Still, maybe not asking was worse.

When the second course was cleared away, he leaned forward.

"I sense a mood," he said gently. "Is everything okay?"

Charlotte's restraint finally cracked.

"Okay?" she echoed, her voice trembling. "Did you even get the flowers?"

Andy froze.

"What flowers?"

"The flowers," she said. "I left them at reception."

"Reception where?"

"At your job. PCP." Her voice broke. "I went there to surprise you. I even wore sexy lingerie, because I thought you might pull me into your office like some ridiculous sexy secretary fantasy."

She wiped her eyes, embarrassed and hurt.

"Do you know how much that bra hurt?" she continued bitterly. "They said they couldn't find you in the system. Then they said something must be wrong. I left the flowers there. At reception."

She looked at him.

"Did nobody give them to you?"

Andy's heart dropped into his stomach.

He took a breath.

"Charlotte," he said quietly.

She shook her head. "That fucking receptionist probably stole them."

"Charlotte," he said again.

He saw how hurt she was. How vulnerable.

He loved her.

And now the moment had ripened.

"Charlotte, listen…" he said.

The words hung between them.

This time, there was no peacock.

No kangaroo.

No interruption.

Only the truth waiting to be spoken.

Chapter 13

THE TRUTH

It was not the ideal moment. But it was the moment. The moment the truth came out.

"Charlotte, listen..."

Andy's voice sounded different now. Lower. Stripped of its practised ease.

She stopped wiping her tears and looked at him, really looked at him, as if bracing herself for impact.

"I need to tell you something," he said. "And I need you to let me finish."

She did not nod. She did not interrupt. She just sat there, hands folded tightly in her lap, eyes glassy and alert.

"I don't work at PCP," Andy said.

The words landed quietly. No drama. No raised voice. Just a sentence that bent the room around it. Like a question mark suspended in air.

Charlotte blinked.

"I don't work there," he repeated. "I never have."

Her face went still, as if something inside her had frozen mid-motion.

"I lied to you," he continued, the words starting to rush now that they had begun. "About my job. About how well I'm doing."

She stared at him, waiting for something else. A correction. A laugh. Anything that would rewind the last ten seconds.

"There is no consulting job," he said. "There is no office. No clients. I've been unemployed since I finished my degree. I live with my mother. I've been looking for work for more than two years."

The silence thickened. Pressed down on the tablecloth, the glasses, their breathing.

"I did it because I was scared," Andy said. "Because I didn't want you to see me like this. Because I didn't think you would stay if you knew. Or like me."

Charlotte let out a sound that was almost a laugh. Sharp. Broken.

"So… the cars?" she asked.

"Your apartment?"

"The dinners?"

"Credit," Andy said, leaning back slightly, as if the word itself weighed something. "Loans. Cards. All of it."

Her breath hitched.

"How much?" she asked, barely audible.

"More than thirty thousand," he said. "I'm drowning in debt."

She pressed a hand to her mouth.

"I'm so sorry," Andy said, again and again. "I'm so sorry, Charlotte."

He reached for her hand. She pulled it away.

"I never meant to hurt you," he said. "I never meant for it to go this far."

He leaned forward, desperation overtaking caution.

Charlotte sat there in shock. In disgust.

"I love you," Andy said. "I have loved you since the first glance. Since the first date. Since the moment you replied to that stupid kangaroo message. My intention towards you was always true. Everything I felt was real."

She shook her head slowly.

She was watching a man turn into a child.

Begging.

Shrinking.

"You don't get to say that," she said. Her voice trembled, but it was steady enough to hurt. "You don't get to tell me what was real."

"I was myself," Andy said, tears running freely now. "Everything else was me. My feelings. My care. My love. The only thing I lied about was..."

"Who you are," she interrupted.

The words cut cleanly.

"You lied about who you are," she said again, louder now. "You let me fall in love with someone who doesn't exist."

"That's not true," Andy said. "I exist. I'm right here. Flesh and blood."

"No," Charlotte said, standing abruptly. Her chair scraped loudly against the floor, drawing glances from nearby tables. "Not like this. You let me trust you. You let me plan a future with you."

Her hands were shaking.

"I told you about my past," she said. "I told you how careful I am. How I don't say I love you easily. And you looked me in the eye and lied."

"I know," Andy said, breaking. "I know. And I hate myself for it. But please, please understand, I did it because I didn't want to lose you."

"That's exactly why it's unforgivable," she said.

Her voice cracked.

"You took my choice away."

Tears spilled freely now, unstoppable. She grabbed her bag, fumbling with the strap.

"I trusted you," she said again, as if trying to convince herself it had been real. "I trusted you."

"Charlotte, please," Andy said, standing as well. "Don't go. Let me fix this. I will fix everything. I have an interview coming up. I'm trying. I swear."

She laughed. Hollow. Raw.

"You don't get to ask me to wait for the truth after lying to me for months," she said.

She turned and walked away from the table, her heels striking the floor too fast, too hard.

"Charlotte!" Andy called.

She didn't turn around.

She pushed through the doors of the Grand Hotel and out into the cold night, without her coat, without looking back, holding her tears in as long as she could.

Andy stood frozen by the table, surrounded by white tablecloths, half-finished glasses, the quiet hum of other people's Valentine's evenings continuing untouched around him.

The truth had finally been spoken.

And it had cost him everything.

Chapter 14

THE LONE WOLF

The room had not changed much since he was seventeen. The same narrow bed. The same desk pressed against the wall. The same Barack Obama poster, now gone, leaving behind a yellowed rectangle where it had once hung, like a scar the wall had learned to live with.

Andy lay on his bed without moving.

The room was dark except for the pale glow of his phone, held a little too close to his face. He scrolled slowly, deliberately, as if moving faster might make the images disappear before he had to feel them.

Charlotte laughing on a street corner.

Charlotte at the zoo, squinting into the sun.

Charlotte half-reflected in a window, caught accidentally, smiling at him.

Photos that now felt illegal to look at. Evidence of a life he no longer had permission to remember. Almost a crime.

It had been a week since the night at the Grand Hotel.

And Andy missed her.

He stopped on a photo taken just before Christmas. Her head tilted against his shoulder, her smile soft and unguarded, his arm wrapped around her waist. He remembered taking it without thinking, pressing the shutter on the phone screen because it felt obvious that moments like that were meant to be kept.

His chest tightened.

Shame arrived first. Heavy. Sticky. The kind that didn't shout, just settled in and pressed inward. Shame for lying. Shame for being exposed. Shame for having believed, however briefly, that it might all work out.

Then panic crept in, mixed with embarrassment.

His thoughts fractured.

What if she told her friends?

What if she told her parents?

What if she never spoke to him again?

He let the phone fall onto his chest and stared at the ceiling. At nothing.

At the place where the poster had once hung. Curled. Peeled. Eventually escaped, leaving only its outline behind.

This room had witnessed every version of him.

Hopeful.

Stalled.

Pretending.

And now it held the wreckage too.

Downstairs, he heard movement. A cupboard opening. A kettle filling.

His mother knew what had happened.

She hadn't asked. She didn't need to.

There was a gentle knock at his door, barely a knock at all.

"Andy?" she said.

Silence.

She opened the door slowly anyway. He didn't turn to look at her.

She stood there for a moment, taking him in. The stillness. The way his body seemed folded inward, as if trying to take up less space.

"I made some tea," she said softly.

No response.

She sat on the edge of the bed, careful not to touch him. The distance between them felt deliberate. Necessary.

"I don't need to ask," she said. "I know what happened."

Andy kept staring at the wall.

"I don't want to talk about it," he said.

She nodded. "Okay."

She stayed anyway.

After a while, she said, "You did something brave."

He let out a short, humourless laugh. "I destroyed everything."

"You told the truth," she replied. "That matters."

"It didn't help," he said. "It just proved I was right to be scared."

"You don't get to decide that yet," she said gently.

"I don't want your optimism," he snapped. "I don't want fixing. I just want to be left alone."

She stood up.

As she turned toward the door, he spoke again.

"It's all your fault," he said. "You told me to tell her."

She stopped.

"Well, it's your fault you lied in the first place," she said sharply, her voice rising now, "and got yourself thirty thousand dollars into debt. So don't put your bad decisions on other people."

Andy turned away from her again.

"I'll be downstairs," she said. "If you need me."

He didn't answer.

When the door closed, the quiet returned, thicker now, more complete.

Andy reached for his phone again. Not for Charlotte. To escape her.

He opened a video app and scrolled until he found voices that felt familiar. Thumbnails of men staring sternly into cameras. Microphones positioned like weapons.

He pressed play.

The room filled with certainty.

Women are hypergamous.

Women only love conditionally.

Men are valued for what they provide.

Andy listened.

At first, it felt like relief. Like someone had handed him an explanation neat enough to wrap his pain in. It wasn't about his lie. It wasn't about his fear. It was about the system. About expectations. About how men like him were set up to fail.

He let the words wash over him.

Each sentence dulled something sharp. Each generalisation created distance from responsibility.

He wasn't broken.

He wasn't dishonest.

He was just naïve.

The voices continued, telling him stories where men were always misunderstood and women always wanted more than they admitted.

It didn't make him feel better.

But it made him feel less alone in his bitterness.

Hours passed unnoticed.

Then his phone buzzed in his hand.

A notification.

His breath caught before he even looked.

Charlotte.

Just one message.

No explanation.

No apology.

No anger.

Dinner. My place. Tomorrow.

Andy stared at the screen in disbelief. His

heart pounded, shame and hope colliding painfully in his chest.

He decided not to answer. He felt he had embarrassed himself too much.

He put the phone down.

Then picked it up again.

What time tomorrow? he wrote.

6 pm, she replied.

Ok, see you.

The room felt suddenly too small.

He didn't know whether it was an ending or a reckoning.

But it was something.

And for now, that was enough to keep him awake.

INTERLUDE 5

Charlotte IV

Charlotte had not meant for a week to pass without speaking to him.

She needed time to process.

It simply happened that way. One unanswered message became two. Two became silence. Silence became a decision she did not remember consciously making.

Andy had written. Long messages. Apologies stacked on top of apologies. Explanations she did not open all the way, previewed just enough to recognise their shape.

I'm sorry...

I didn't mean to...

Please let me explain...

She left them unread, as if keeping them unopened preserved something fragile inside her. As if opening them would collapse whatever structure she was barely holding together.

Instead, she talked to her friends.

Mostly, she talked to Sabrina.

They did something Sabrina called wine-therapy. They drank wine on Sabrina's sofa, legs tucked beneath them, glasses refilled too often. An essential part of the therapy, according to Sabrina.

They dissected the situation carefully.

Then carelessly.

Then emotionally.

"He lied to you," Sabrina said. "For months."

"I know," Charlotte replied, slamming her drunken hand against her forehead.

"That's not a small thing."

"I know."

"And the money thing…"

"I know."

The words I know came too easily. Too smoothly. Because knowing was not the problem.

Feeling was.

"But Sabrina," Charlotte said, her voice breaking, "I love him. Or I loved him. And I'm in so much pain I can't even describe it. It's worse than childbirth."

She collapsed into tears, dramatic and uncontained, letting herself go completely.

"Hey, Charlie," Sabrina interrupted gently, half-laughing, half-concerned. "You need to let it go. Let the broke guy go. And also… you've never given birth. How would you know?"

A laugh broke through the crying. Then more I knows followed.

Somewhere along the way, Andy had shifted

from the finance guy to the broke guy in Sabrina's internal system of nicknames.

Charlotte knew, with a tired kind of certainty, that something bad always followed when she fell in love. Not because love itself was dangerous, but because it softened her. Made her hopeful. Made her willing to believe in futures before they were earned.

She had seen the pattern before. Trusted too quickly. Invested deeply. Built entire inner lives around people who could not, or would not, hold them.

Her mind drifted back to her first first love. Elementary school. A boy named Trevor in the parallel class.

She had told him she loved him. He had said he loved her back. Back then, love was thrown around easily, like a promise that didn't yet know its weight.

They decided to get married on the playground. Ten a.m. sharp.

Charlotte had been radiant with excitement. She had even taken her mother's weeding tiara to wear on her wedding day.

When she arrived, Trevor was marrying Tracy instead. The ceremony was officiated by Ed, a boy from her class.

Charlotte hid in the bushes and cried for the rest of the day. Missed class. Got her parents called in. Her first heartbreak, complete and theatrical. But at the same time real.

But this is different, she told herself now.

That was always the most dangerous thought.

At night, she replayed moments, not the glamorous ones, but the small, ordinary ones. Andy listening when she spoke. Andy holding her when she went quiet, without asking her to explain herself.

She felt foolish for missing those things. Angry at herself for missing them.

And angry at him.

The anger surprised her with its intensity. It was sharp, persistent, alive in a way disappointment alone never was. It took her days to understand why.

She was angry because she still loved him.

If she had stopped loving him, the lie would have settled neatly into place. A lesson. A story to tell later. A warning sign she had ignored.

But love complicated everything.

Love made her want to understand instead of condemning. Love made her curious when she wanted to be done. Love made her imagine Andy not as a villain, but as someone frightened enough to destroy something good before it could leave him.

She hated that part of herself. The part that empathised.

She went for long walks alone, letting the city absorb her restlessness. She passed couples holding hands and felt nothing. She passed places she and Andy had been and felt too much.

One afternoon, she saw a small child walking between two parents, hands held tightly. The sight made her stop and cry unexpectedly.

What if that could have been me and Andy?

She told herself, firmly, that forgiveness did not mean forgetting. That understanding did not mean excusing. That loving someone did not obligate her to stay.

But it did obligate her, to herself, to know the truth of her feelings.

Avoidance had given her distance.

It had not given her clarity.

One evening, sitting at her kitchen table with a cup of tea gone cold, she admitted what she had been circling for days:

She wanted to see him.

Not to forgive him immediately. Not to promise anything. Just to sit across from him without wine-therapy, without friends, without noise. To see whether what she felt in his presence still matched what lingered in his absence.

To see whether love was still there, or whether it had finally begun to loosen its grip.

She picked up her phone.

The thread of his messages sat there, unread but present, like something alive but waiting.

She did not read them.

She did not explain.

She typed only what she could commit to:

Dinner. My place. Tomorrow.

She stared at the screen longer than necessary.

Then she pressed send.

Whatever happened next, she decided, would

happen with her eyes open.

Chapter 15

THE DINNER

Andy was terrified to meet Charlotte that evening. It felt like being summoned to court, to stand before someone who already knew the verdict, waiting only to announce the punishment. As if this dinner was not a conversation, but a sentence.

He had decided to be truly honest. Fully. Not strategically honest, not partially honest, honest in the way that left no place to hide. His goal was simple and impossible at the same time: to show her how much he loved her and to win her back.

It felt harder now than it ever had on Tinder.

He stood outside her apartment door for a moment longer than necessary, taking in the stillness, like a criminal hesitating before entering the courtroom.

He rang the bell.

Charlotte opened the door, holding back her smile as much as possible.

She wasn't trying to be cold. She was careful.

As if she had decided not to waste energy pretending, she was somewhere she wasn't.

Andy stood there holding nothing. No flowers. No gifts. Just himself, stripped of all the performances he had relied on for months. That felt intentional. Necessary.

"Hi," he said.

"Hi," she replied, stepping aside.

Her apartment smelled like food and something citrusy, clean. The table was already set. Simple. No candles. No ceremony. Two plates. Two glasses. Water poured.

They sat across from each other.

For a moment, neither of them spoke.

Charlotte broke the silence.

"I need to understand," she said. "Not the facts. I know the facts. I need to understand why you did what you did."

Andy nodded.

After a pause, he said, "I feel like a loser."

The word hung there, unfiltered.

"Like a nobody who didn't deserve anything good," he continued. "I felt like a failure who had done everything right on paper and still ended up nowhere. Stuck. Living at my mother's place..."

"There's nothing wrong with living at your mother's place," Charlotte interrupted gently. "I lived with my parents for a year until I found a job here."

"You don't understand," he said quickly, eager not to lose his thread. "I have no job. No money.

No future that makes sense. Only a diploma for a master's in business administration. Nothing."

She listened without interrupting.

"When I met you," he continued, "you felt... complete. Like someone who had actually arrived somewhere in life. I was terrified you'd look at me and see exactly what I was afraid of seeing myself."

"So you invented someone else," she said quietly. "You know I'm not perfect either. We could have met each other in our imperfections."

"Yes," Andy said. "At first it felt small. A title. A sentence. Something I could fix later. But every time I didn't tell the truth, it became harder to do it the next time."

He paused.

"I was going to tell you on our first date," he said. "But it felt like momentum. And I didn't want to stop it."

He looked down at his hands.

"I hated myself for it. Every single day. But I love you more than I hate the lie. Or at least... I thought I did."

Charlotte leaned back in her chair.

"That's the problem, Andy," she said. "Love doesn't grow by protecting yourself from the truth."

He nodded.

"I know."

They ate in silence for a while. The food was good. Cooked with care. Neither of them commented on it.

Then Charlotte spoke again.

"You know," she said, "my first love was when I was a kid. Elementary school. I told him I loved him. He said it back. We planned a fake child wedding on the playground."

She let out a small, humourless laugh and stared into the distance.

"I took it seriously. I brought my mother's wedding tiara."

Andy smiled faintly, then stopped when he saw her serious face.

"He married someone else that same day."

She took a sip of her water glass.

"It sounds ridiculous," she said. "But it broke something early. Taught me that love can disappear without warning."

She paused.

"My second love was in high school. That one was real. Long. Serious. I built myself into his family, his future. And one day he just..." she clapped her hands once "...decided he was done."

Andy recognised the look in her eyes. The way grief settles and never quite leaves.

"So when I said I love you," she continued, "it wasn't impulsive. It was terrifying. And you lied to me in the moment where I needed reality the most."

"I know," Andy said. "And I'm truly sorry. I know sorry isn't enough."

"No," she said. "It isn't."

Later, they moved to the sofa. Not touching at first. Then closer. Then without thinking about it.

"I don't know what I'm feeling," Charlotte said

quietly. "Everything feels strange now."

Andy stayed silent.

"You gave me so much these past months," she continued. "A relationship. Love. A caring, generous man. I have appreciated that."

"I know," Andy said, breaking. "And it makes it worse."

"And all along," she said softly, "you were insincere with me."

"I didn't want to be," he said quickly. "I just wanted to match a standard set by others. As a man, I thought I had to provide. Be successful."

She shushed him gently.

"I know," she said. "It's a mess."

She kissed him, softly. A kiss that felt new. Careful. Nothing like before.

"Can you hold me tonight?" she asked. "Just... hold me."

Andy did.

They slept in the same bed, bodies familiar but something essential shifted. He noticed it. She did too. Neither of them named it. It felt like sleeping beside a stranger you cared deeply about.

In the morning, the light felt different.

Charlotte sat on the edge of the bed, wrapped in the sheet, staring out the window.

"This feels different," she said. "Strange."

Andy's chest tightened.

"Not bad," she added. "Just... not like before."

He stayed quiet.

"I think we need a pause," she said. "Not because I don't care. But because I need to know whether what I'm feeling is real, or just habit."

"I understand," he said, though he wasn't sure he did.

She looked at him then. Really looked at him.

"I still love you," she said. "That's the problem."

She stood, pulled on a sweater, and kissed his cheek, not his mouth.

"Let's not break this by forcing it," she said softly.

Andy left shortly after.

More heartbroken than before. More confused.

Outside, the city went on as it always did.

And Andy realised something quietly devastating:

Losing her all at once would have been easier than losing her slowly, honestly, and by degrees.

Chapter 16

THE PAUSE

The pause did not feel like a relief.

Andy had imagined it might. A break. A breath. Time to fix things quietly, efficiently, the way problems were supposed to be fixed. Instead, it felt like standing on the edge of something that had already begun to crumble, pretending it was still solid ground.

They had not defined the pause. That was the problem.

It had been a month since the dinner.

Andy had been jumping through hoops in his application to PCP. Interviews. Case studies. Workshops. Each step felt like proof that what he had imagined for himself was finally within reach.

He felt hopeful. Too hopeful.

Charlotte did not disappear completely. She sent polite messages: short, careful, considerate.

Hope you're okay.

Busy week.

How are you?

Messages that acknowledged his existence without inviting him back into her life.

Andy replied in the same tone. Neutral. Controlled. As if language itself could bruise if handled too roughly.

They did not see each other.

Andy filled the space with activity. Or tried to.

He reread old university books, forcing himself back into finance theory and consulting frameworks, as if memory alone could substitute for experience.

The debts did not pause.

Credit piled up. Late fees followed. Numbers grew quietly, patiently.

He told himself it would all make sense once he got the job.

The letters arrived faster now. Red text. Thicker envelopes. Final notices that no longer pretended to be polite.

His mother noticed that something was moving forward, but that Andy was somehow feeling worse than the day before.

They moved around each other carefully, both aware that the house had become a place of quiet emergencies. She tried to talk to him once, about Charlotte, about the money, but he shut it down before it could begin.

"Let me be, Mum," he said.

At night, he lay awake replaying moments not as they had happened, but as they could have gone differently. Versions of himself who told the truth earlier. Versions of Charlotte who stayed. Futures that branched off and vanished the moment he tried to hold onto them.

He stopped listening to the podcasts. Their certainty felt hollow now, unable to compete with the specificity of his loss.

Charlotte, meanwhile, tried to live normally.

She threw herself into work. The children were loud, immediate, forgiving. They demanded her full presence, which left little room for spiraling thoughts during the day. In the evenings, the silence returned.

She told herself the pause was necessary. Healthy. Mature.

But she missed him in ways that surprised her. Missed the way he listened. Missed his hands. Missed the version of herself she had been with him: open, hopeful, less guarded.

In love.

Still.

She also felt angry.

Angry that loving him had cost her certainty. Angry that she had been forced to choose between protecting herself and holding onto something that had felt real.

She wondered whether love was supposed to feel this exhausting.

It always seemed to be.

They passed each other once in the city. By accident. Across a street.

Andy saw her first.

She was standing on the opposite pavement, laughing with a friend, head tilted back slightly, hair loose beneath her coat. Her coat was open despite the cold, as if she had forgotten about it. She looked unguarded. Alive.

The sight of her hit him physically, a tightness in his chest that stole his breath for a moment. Not longing exactly, something heavier. A recognition of what had been lost before it was fully understood.

She did not see him.

Andy stood still, suddenly conscious of himself in a way that felt almost humiliating. The angle of his shoulders. The stiffness in his stance. The way his coat hung on him, chosen carefully once, now rags. He felt exposed, as if his lack of purpose were visible on his skin.

He imagined what she saw instead.

A future unfolding without friction. A version of herself moving forward, laughing freely, unburdened by his uncertainty, his debt, his apologies. A life in which love had been painful but survivable. A life that did not circle back to him.

Something collapsed quietly in his chest then. Not all at once. Just a small internal surrender, like a structure giving way under weight it had carried too long.

He could cross the street. Say her name.

He did not.

He stayed where he was, rooted to the pavement, watching the light change, watching her turn slightly, watching the moment pass without touching him.

Then he turned away before she could look up.

And as he walked, he felt himself shrink, not just in her absence, but in his own.

Later in the day, he received the email from PCP.

A rejection.

After weeks of interviews, assessments, polite enthusiasm, and language that suggested possibility, the email was brief and clean:

We've decided to move forward with other candidates.

No explanation. No feedback. No acknowledgment of the effort it had taken just to remain visible.

Andy stared at the screen for a long time.

PCP had been the story he told himself when everything else fell apart. The justification. The proof that he could still become the man he pretended to be. Without it, there was nothing left to point toward.

He felt exposed. Stripped.

A man without work. Without money. Without direction.

A man who could not provide.

A man who had nothing to offer except apologies.

Worthless.

A failure.

That night, Andy drank alone in his room. Not heavily. Just enough to blur the edges of things. He stared at the yellowed rectangle on the wall where the Barack Obama poster had once hung, thinking about permanence. About how even absence left marks.

The idea came quietly.

Not as a plan. Not as despair.

As a thought that felt almost practical. Logical.

If I disappear, the noise stops.

The debts.

The explanations.

The waiting.

The phase.

The pause.

The guilt.

The anxiety.

The worthlessness.

The embarrassment.

He dismissed it at first. Then again. Then less firmly.

Days blurred into weeks.

Charlotte noticed her messages were no longer being opened.

She considered calling him. Many times. Each time she told herself that if he needed her, he would reach out. That the pause was mutual. That silence was part of the agreement she had never articulated.

Andy, meanwhile, felt himself shrinking.

Not suddenly, but steadily, like something being quietly compressed. He spoke less, not because he had nothing to say, but because words felt like claims he could no longer justify. He avoided mirrors. Avoided rooms where his presence might require explanation. Even his thoughts arrived already apologising for taking up space.

He stopped going to the unemployment agency.

Not out of defiance, but humiliation. Sitting there among other men his age, some older, some younger, waiting in silence to be processed made him feel exposed in a way he could not endure. Men who were meant to be providers, planners, forward-moving. Men who were supposed to turn effort into outcome. Each visit reinforced the same message: he had failed at the one thing he had been taught mattered.

He stayed home instead.

He told himself he would go tomorrow. Tomorrow became a word without obligation.

He stopped opening letters. At first he stacked them neatly, then shoved them into drawers, then stopped touching them at all. Red print. Final notices. Language that no longer pretended to be polite. The numbers were no longer shocking, just proof of something irreversible. He told himself unread problems were suspended problems, as if reality required his consent.

He stopped imagining futures that required endurance.

Futures where he rebuilt himself slowly. Where he started again at the bottom. Where he had to explain, to Charlotte, to his mother, to himself, why he was still not enough. The idea of "working towards something" began to feel like a cruelty reserved for people who still believed they were worth the effort.

The world narrowed into manageable units: morning, afternoon, night.

Wake. Scroll. Eat. Sleep.

Days were no longer lived inside; they were survived.

He cleaned his room obsessively.

He threw away old university notebooks filled with ambition, with plans written in the confident handwriting of someone who believed effort would be rewarded. He folded clothes he no longer wore, smoothing them with unnecessary care, arranging them as if someone else might one day need to go through his things.

He wiped surfaces that were already clean.

Straightened objects that did not need straightening.

These were not acts of renewal.

They were acts of erasure.

Small, deliberate reductions. Clearing space. Leaving less behind. Making himself easier to remove.

When he finally sat down on the edge of his bed, the room felt larger. Emptier.

And Andy felt what he had been feeling for weeks now, without language for it:

Useless.

Replaceable.

Already gone.

That same day, Charlotte visited her doctor.

She received news.

When she was asleep that night, she dreamed of Andy. Not dramatically. Just sitting beside her: quiet, present, real. Holding her. Kissing her.

She woke with a heaviness she could not explain.

As if something bad was about to happen.

She picked up her phone.

Typed his name.

Paused.

Put it down again.

She was holding a piece of news she knew mattered. News that felt too important for a message.

She decided it could wait until morning.

She would go to his mother's place. Tell him in person.

Chapter 17

THE END

Andy woke up with a strange calm.

Not relief exactly, something quieter than that. Certainty. The kind that settles when questions have exhausted themselves. When every alternative has already been rehearsed and dismissed.

He did not dress.

He walked around the house in his underwear.

The house was empty. His mother was already gone. Morning moved through the rooms without resistance. Light through windows. Air that felt clean and indifferent.

He turned on the bath and headed for the cellar, already committed to the order of things.

The cellar had always felt separate from the rest of the home. Cooler. Dimmer. A place where things were stored and forgotten. He moved through it carefully, methodically, as if following a routine he had rehearsed without ever admitting it to himself.

He interfered with the house's electric safeguards, making sure nothing would interrupt what he had already decided. Disabling the last protection that might have stopped him. He did not hesitate.

He did not think in words anymore. Not in sentences. Only in conclusions.

Upstairs, the house remained unaware.

He placed the toaster from the kitchen, plugged in, beside the tub with deliberate care, the way people do when they want to convince themselves they are still rational. Still in control.

The bathroom filled with steam. The mirror softened his reflection until it no longer demanded recognition. He stepped into the water and let himself sink into the stillness.

There was no revelation.

Only quiet.

The kind of quiet that arrives when the noise finally stops arguing.

He picked up the toaster and held it over his body.

He was not scared.

He had decided this.

Charlotte was already on her way.

She had woken with resolve she hadn't felt in weeks. Something had settled overnight. Not certainty, but readiness.

She had thought about Andy carefully. About fear disguised as pride. About shame masquerading as control. About how love, when mixed with expectation, can turn into performance.

She still loved him.

That truth had survived anger, distance, and silence.

The news she carried felt too important for a text message. Too fragile for interpretation. She wanted to say it aloud. Wanted to look at him when she did.

She took the bus to his mother's house, rehearsing nothing specific, only honesty. Slowly. Gently. Without illusions.

She told herself she was doing the right thing.

In the bathroom, Andy lay still. Holding the toaster above him.

The water had reached the point where everything felt distant, dulled. The air was heavy. Time had lost its shape.

Then he heard a sound.

A knock.

It came from far away, from the front door. He ignored it.

Another knock.

More insistent.

He closed his eyes.

A voice followed. Calling his name. Familiar. Urgent.

"Andy!"

He recognised it, dimly

He did not move. He continued with his mission.

He dropped the toaster in the water.

As he shook in the bathtub, electrocuted.

The knocking continued.

His name again.

In his last moment of consciousness, he realised:

It was Charlotte.

Andy made no sound.

He was on a path away from this world.

Following the light, that so many talk about.

Into the light.

He went.

The light.

Becoming brighter with every step.

He escaped.

Charlotte knocked harder now.

She understood something was not right.

"Andy?" she called, her voice tightening. "Andy!"

The house did not answer.

She reached for her phone and called his number.

Three hollow tones followed.

The number was no longer in service.

Her breath caught.

She knocked harder.

Andy had gone into the light.

It was quiet.

Too quiet.

Not peaceful.

Settled

The kind of quiet that does not resolve, only remains.

THE END.

ABOUT THE AUTHOR

Nikita Zabzine

Nikita Zabzine is a Swedish author whose debut novel, Too Good To Be True, explores the emotional and financial pressures facing a generation raised on promises of success in an increasingly unstable world.

Born in St Petersburg, Russia, in 1996, Nikita grew up across Europe — living in Italy, France, Great Britain, Russia, and Sweden — as his parents worked at various universities. This international upbringing shaped his perspective on identity, ambition, and belonging in contemporary society.

He studied philosophy at Stockholm University, where he developed a deep interest in truth, self-perception, and the narratives people construct to navigate social expectations. His writing blends romance, psychological tension, and sharp social observation to examine the hidden costs of performance culture, economic insecurity, and modern masculinity.

Too Good To Be True is his first published work.

www.ingramcontent.com/pod-product-compliance
Lightning Source LLC
LaVergne TN
LVHW051003080826
845145LV00009B/2439

9789153185659